KU-276-934

THE PLAYBOY
OF ROME

THE PLAYBOY OF ROME

BY

JENNIFER FAYE

MILLS & BOON®

First published in Great Britain 2015
by Mills & Boon, an imprint of Harlequin (UK) Limited,
Large Print edition 2015
Eton House, 18-24 Paradise Road,
Richmond, Surrey, TW9 1SR

© 2015 Jennifer F. Stroka

ISBN: 978-0-263-25656-7

Harlequin (UK) Limited's policy is to use papers that are natural, renewable and recyclable products and made from wood grown in sustainable forests. The logging and manufacturing processes conform to the legal environmental regulations of the country of origin.

Printed and bound in Great Britain
by CPI Antony Rowe, Chippenham, Wiltshire

For Ami.

To a wonderful friend who has kept me
company as we've walked a similar path.

Thank you for your friendship
and unwavering encouragement.

CHAPTER ONE

"SCUSA."

Dante DeFiore stepped into the path of a young woman trying to skirt around the line at Ristorante Massimo. Her long blond hair swished over her shoulder as she turned to him. Her icy blue gaze met his. The impact of her piercing stare rocked him. He couldn't turn away. Thick black eyeliner and sky-blue eye shadow that shimmered succeeded in making her stunning eyes even more extraordinary.

Dante cleared his throat. "Signorina, are you meeting someone?"

"No, I'm not."

"Really?" He truly was surprised. "Someone as beautiful as you shouldn't be alone."

Her fine brows rose and a smile tugged at her tempting lips.

He smiled back. Any other time, he'd have been happy to ask her to be his personal guest but not tonight. Inwardly he groaned. Why did he have to have his hands full juggling both positions of maître d' and head chef when the most delicious creature was standing in front of him?

He choked down his regret. It just wasn't meant to be. Tonight there was no time for flirting—not even with this stunning woman who could easily turn heads on the runways of Milan.

He glanced away from her in order to clear his thoughts. Expectant looks from the people waiting to be seated reminded him of his duties. He turned back to those amazing blue eyes. "I hate to say this, but you'll have to take your place at the end of the line."

"It's okay." Her pink glossy lips lifted into a knowing smile. "You don't have to worry. I work here."

"Here?" Impossible. He'd certainly remember her. By the sounds of her speech, she was American.

"This is Mr. Bianco's restaurant, isn't it?"

"Yes, it is."

"Then I'm in the right place."

Suddenly the pieces fell into place. His staff had been cut in half because of a nasty virus running rampant throughout Rome. He'd called around to see if any business associates could loan him an employee or two. Apparently when Luigi said he might be able to track down a friend of one of his daughters, he'd gotten lucky.

Relief flooded through Dante. Help was here at last and by the looks of her, she'd certainly be able to draw in the crowds. Not so long ago, they hadn't needed anyone to draw in customers; his grandfather's cooking was renowned through-out Rome. But in recent months all of that had changed.

"And I'd be the luckiest man in the world to have such a beauty working here. You'll have the men lined up down the street. Just give me a mo-ment." Dante turned and signaled to the waiter.

When Michael approached Dante, the man's forehead was creased in confusion. "What do you need?"

In that moment, Dante's mind drew a blank. All he could envision were those mesmerizing blue eyes. This was ridiculous. He had a business to run.

When he glanced over at the line of customers at the door, the anxious stares struck a chord in his mind. "Michael, could you seat that couple over there?" He pointed to an older couple. "Give them the corner table. It's their fortieth anniversary, so make sure their meal is on us."

"No *problema*."

Lines of exhaustion bracketed Michael's mouth. Dante couldn't blame the guy. Being shorthanded and having to see to the dining room himself was a lot of work.

Dante turned his attention back to his unexpected employee. She had her arms crossed and her slender hip hitched to the side. A slight smile pulled at the corners of her lush lips as though she knew she'd caught him off guard—something that rarely happened to him.

He started to smile back when a patron entered the door and called out a greeting, reminding Dante that work came first. Since his grandfather was no longer around to help shoulder the burden of running this place, Dante's social life had been reduced to interaction with the guests of Ristorante Massimo.

After a brief *ciao* to a regular patron, Dante turned back to his temporary employee. "Thanks for coming. If you give me your coat, I can hang it up for you."

"I've got it." She clutched the lapels but made no attempt to take it off.

"You can hang it over there." He pointed to the small cloakroom. "We can work out everything later."

"You want me to start right now?"

That was the plan, but perhaps Luigi had failed to make that part clear. "Didn't he tell you that you'd be starting right away?"

"Yes, but I thought I'd have a chance to look around. And I didn't think I'd be a hostess."

"Consider this an emergency. I promise you it's not hard. I'm certain you'll be fantastic…uh…" Did she give him her name? If she had, he couldn't recall it. "What did you say your name is?"

"Lizzie. Lizzie Addler."

"Well, Lizzie, it's a pleasure to meet you. I'm Dante. And I really appreciate you pitching in during this stressful time."

"Are you sure you want me out here? I'd be a lot more help in the kitchen."

The kitchen? With her looks, who would hide such a gem behind closed doors? Perhaps she was just shy. Not that anything about her stunning appearance said that she was an introvert.

"I'd really appreciate it if you could help these people find a table."

She nodded.

An assistant rushed out of the kitchen. "We need you."

By the harried look on the young man's face, Dante knew it couldn't be good. He turned to his new employee. There would be time for introductions and formalities later. Right now, he just needed to keep the kitchen from falling behind and giving the patrons an excuse to look for food elsewhere.

"Sorry for this rush but I am very shorthanded." When the girl sent him a puzzled look, he realized that Luigi might not have filled her in on the details of her duties. "If you could just get everyone seated and get their drinks, Michael can take their orders. Can you do that?"

She nodded before slipping off her long black coat to reveal a frilly white blouse that hinted at her willowy figure, a short black skirt that showed off her long legs and a pair of knee-high sleek black boots. He stifled a whistle. Definitely not the reaction a boss should give an employee, even if she was gorgeous enough to create a whirlwind of excitement on the cover of a fashion magazine.

He strode to the kitchen, hoping that nothing had caught fire and that no one had been injured. When was this evening going to end? And had his grandfather's friend Luigi been trying to help by sending Lizzie? Or trying to drive him to distraction?

Once the kitchen was again humming along, he retraced his steps just far enough to catch a glimpse of the blonde bombshell. She moved about on those high-heeled boots as if they were a natural extension of her long legs. He swallowed hard as his eyes followed her around the dining room. He assured himself that he was just doing his duty by checking up on her.

When she smiled and chatted with a couple of older gentlemen, Dante's gut tightened. She sure seemed far more at ease with those men than when he'd been talking with her. How strange. Usually he didn't have a problem making conversation with the female gender. Lizzie was certainly different. Too bad she wouldn't be around long enough to learn more about her. She intrigued him.

Obviously there was a misunderstanding.

Lizzie Addler frowned as she locked the front door of Ristorante Massimo. She hadn't flown from New York to Italy to be a hostess. She was here to work in the kitchen—to learn from the legendary chef, Massimo Bianco. And to film a television segment to air on the culinary channel's number-one-rated show. It was a dream come true.

The strange thing was she'd flown in two days early, hoping to get her bearings in this new country. How in the world did this Dante know she was going to show up this evening?

It was impossible. But then again, this smooth-talking man seemed to know who she was. So why put her on hostess duty when he knew that her true talents lay in the kitchen?

Her cheeks ached from smiling so much, but all it took was recalling Dante's flattering words and the corners of her lips lifted once again. She'd heard rumors that Italian men were known to be charmers and now that she knew that it was true—at least in Dante's case—she'd have to be careful around him. She couldn't lose focus on her mission here.

She leaned her back against the door and sighed. She couldn't remember the last time her feet ached this much. Why in the world had she decided to wear her new boots today of all days?

Oh, yes, to make a good impression. And technically the boots weren't new—just new to her.

They were secondhand, like all of Lizzie's things. But in her defense, some of her things still had the tags on them when she'd found them at the gently used upscale boutique. And boy, was she thankful she'd splurged on the stylish clothes.

Her gaze strayed to the wall full of framed pictures of celebrities. There were black and whites as well as color photos through the years. Massimo was in a lot of them alongside movie stars, singers and politicians from around the world. As Lizzie scanned the many snapshots, she found Dante's handsome face. In each photo of him, he was smiling broadly with his arm around a beautiful woman.

"Pretty impressive?"

She knew without looking that it'd be Dante. "Very impressive." She forced her gaze to linger on the army of photos instead of rushing to ogle the tall, dark and undeniably handsome man at her side. "Have all of these people eaten here?"

"Yes. And there are more photos back in the office. We ran out of space out here." His voice was distinguishable with its heavy Italian accent. The rich tones flowed through her as seductively as crème brûlée. "We should add your photo."

"Me." She pressed a hand to her chest. "But I'm a nobody."

"You, my dear, are definitely not a nobody." His gaze met hers and heat rushed to her cheeks. "Is everything wrapped up out here?"

Her mouth went dry and she struggled to swallow. "Yes…yes, the last customer just left."

Lines of exhaustion etched the tanned skin around his dark eyes. His lips were lifted in a friendly smile, but something told her that it was all for her benefit and that he didn't feel like doing anything but calling it a night.

"I can't thank you enough for your help this evening." His gaze connected with hers, making her pulse spike. "I suppose you'll be wanting your pay so that you can be on your way. If you would just wait a moment."

Before she could formulate words, he turned and headed to the back of the restaurant. Pay her? For what? Playing hostess for the evening? She supposed that was above and beyond her contract negotiations with the television network.

Dante quickly returned and placed some euros in her hand. His fingers were warm as the backs of his fingers brushed over her palm, causing her stomach to quiver. She quickly pulled her hand away.

"Thank you so much. You truly were a life-saver." He moved to the door to let her out.

She didn't follow him. She wasn't done here. Not by a long shot. "I'm not leaving. Not yet."

Dante shot her a puzzled look. "If this is about the money, this is the amount I told Luigi I was willing to pay—"

Lizzie shook her head. "It's not that. I came here to meet with Chef Massimo."

"You did? You mean Luigi didn't send you?"

"I don't know any Luigi."

Dante reached in his pocket and pulled out his smartphone. A few keystrokes later, he glanced up. "My mistake. Luigi wasn't able to find any-one to help out. Thank goodness you showed up."

"And I was happy to help. Now if you could in-troduce me to Chef Massimo."

Dante's forehead creased. "That's not going to happen." His tone was firm and unbendable. "He's not here. You'll have to deal with me."

"I don't think so. I'll wait for him."

Dante rubbed the back of his neck and sighed. "You'll be waiting a long time. Chef Massimo is out of town."

"Listen, I know I'm here a couple of days ahead of time, but we do have an agreement to meet."

"That's impossible." Dante's shoulders straightened and his expression grew serious. "I would have known. I know about everything that has to do with this place."

"Obviously not in this case." Lizzie pressed her lips together, immediately regretting her outburst. She was tired after her long flight and then having to work all evening as a hostess.

"You're obviously mixed up. You should be going." He pulled open the front door, letting a cool evening breeze sweep inside and wrap around her.

She couldn't leave. Her whole future was riding on this internship, and the money from participating in the upcoming cooking show would pay for her sister's grad school. She couldn't let her down. She'd promised Jules that if she got accepted to graduate school she'd make sure there was money for the tuition. Jules had already had so many setbacks in her life that Lizzie refused to fail her.

She stepped up to Dante, and even though she was wearing heeled boots, she still had to tilt her chin upward to look him in the eyes. "I did you a big favor tonight. The least you can do is hear me out."

Dante let the door swing shut and led her back to the dining room, where he pulled out a chair for her before he took a seat across the table. "I'm listening."

Lizzie wished it wasn't so late in the evening. Dante looked wiped out, not exactly the optimal position to gain his understanding. Still, she didn't have any other place to go.

Her elbows pressed down on the white linen tablecloth as she folded her hands together. "Chef Massimo has agreed to mentor me."

Dante's gaze narrowed in on her. "Why is this the first I'm hearing of it?"

"Why should you know about it? My agreement isn't with you."

"Massimo Bianco is my maternal grandfather. And with him away, I'm running this place."

This man wasn't about to give an inch, at least not easily. "When will he return so we can straighten things out?"

Dante leaned back in his chair and folded his arms. His dark eyes studied her. She'd love to know what he was thinking. Then again, maybe not. The past couple of days had been nothing but a blur. She'd rushed to wrap up her affairs in New York City before catching a transatlantic flight. The last thing she'd wanted to do was play hostess, but she figured she'd be a good sport. After all, Dante seemed to be in a really tight spot. But now she didn't understand why he was being so closemouthed about Massimo.

"All you need to know is that my grandfather won't be returning. So any business you have with him, you'll have to deal with me. Tell me about this agreement."

Uneasiness crept down her spine. This man had disbelief written all over his handsome features. But what choice did she have but to deal with him since she had absolutely no idea how to contact Chef Massimo? The only phone number she had was for this restaurant. And the email had also been for the restaurant.

"The agreement is for him to mentor me for the next two months."

Dante shook his head. "It isn't going to happen. I'm sorry you traveled all of this way for nothing. But you'll have to leave now."

Lizzie hadn't flown halfway around the globe just to be turned away—she'd been rejected too many times in her life. Her reasons for being here ran deeper than appearing on the television show. She truly wanted to learn from the best and Massimo Bianco was a renowned chef, whose name on her résumé would carry a lot of weight in the culinary world.

"Surely you could use the extra help." After what she'd witnessed this evening, she had no doubt about it.

"If not for this virus going around, Massimo's would be fully staffed. We don't have room for someone else in the kitchen."

"Obviously Chef Bianco doesn't agree with your assessment. He assured me there would be a spot for me."

Dante's eyes darkened. "He was mistaken. And now that I've heard you out, I must insist that you leave."

These days she proceeded cautiously and was always prepared. She reached in her oversize purse and pulled out the signed document. "You can't turn me away."

When she held out a copy of the contract, Dante's dark brows rose. Suddenly he didn't look as in charge as he had just a few seconds ago. Funny how a binding legal document could change things so quickly.

When he reached for the papers, their fingers brushed. His skin was warm and surprisingly smooth. Their gazes met and held. His eyes were dark and mysterious. Instead of being intimidated by him, she was drawn to him.

Not that she was in Italy to have a summer romance. She had a job to do and this man was standing between her and her future. He may be stubborn, but he'd just met his match.

CHAPTER TWO

WHAT WAS IT about this woman that had him feeling off-kilter?

Could it be the way her touch sent currents of awareness up his arm? Realizing they were still touching, Dante jerked his hand away. He clenched his fingers, creasing the hefty document.

Or maybe it was those cool blue eyes of hers that seemed to study his every move. It was as though she could see more of him than he cared for anyone to observe. Not that he had any secrets to hide—well, other than his plans to sell the *ristorante*.

His gaze scrolled over the first lines of the document, pausing when he saw his grandfather's name followed by Ristorante Massimo. He continued skimming over the legalese until his gaze screeched to a halt at the mention of a television show. His gut twisted into a knot. This was much more involved than he'd ever imagined.

"You said this was for an internship. You didn't mention anything about a television show."

Her lips moved but nothing came out. It was as though she wasn't sure exactly how to proceed. If she thought he was going to make this easy for her, she'd have to think again. She'd tried to get him to agree to let her work here under false pretenses when in fact she had much bigger plans.

When she didn't respond fast enough, he added, "How long were you planning to keep that little bit of information a secret?"

Her forehead wrinkled. "Obviously I wasn't keeping it a secret or I wouldn't have handed you the contract."

She had a valid point, but it didn't ease his agitation. He once again rubbed at his stiff neck. It'd been an extremely long day. Not only was he short-staffed but also the meeting with the potential buyers for the *ristorante* hadn't gone well. They didn't just want the building. They also wanted the name and the secret recipes that put his grandfather's name up there with the finest chefs.

Dante didn't have the right to sell those recipes—recipes that went back to his grandmother's time. They were special to his grandfather. Still, selling them would keep them alive for others to enjoy instead of them being forgotten in a drawer. But could he actually approach his grandfather and ask for the right to sell them? Those recipes were his grandfather's pride and joy. In fact, employees signed a nondisclosure agreement to maintain the secrecy of Massimo's signature dishes. The thought of selling out left a sour taste in Dante's mouth.

"As you can see in the contract, the television crew will be here on Tuesday." Her words brought Dante back to his latest problem.

"I also see that you've arrived a couple of days early." He wasn't sure what he meant by that statement. He was stalling. Thinking.

"I like to be prepared. I don't like surprises. So I thought I'd get settled in and maybe see some of the sights in Rome. I've heard it's a lovely city."

"Well, since my grandfather isn't going to be able to mentor you, perhaps you can have an extended holiday before heading back to—"

"New York. And I didn't come here for a vacation. I came here to work and to learn." She got to her feet. "Maybe I should just speak with one of the people in the kitchen. Perhaps they can point me in the direction of your grandfather."

"That won't be necessary."

His grandfather didn't need to be bothered with this—he had more important issues to deal with at the moment. Dante could and would handle this woman. After all, there had to be a way out of this. Without reading the rest of the lengthy details, he flipped to the last page.

"It's all signed and legal, if that's what you're worried about." Her voice held a note of confidence, and she sat back down.

She was right. Right there in black and white was his grandfather's distinguished signature. There was no denying the slope of the *M* or the scroll of *Bianco*. Dante resisted the urge to ball up the document and toss it into the stone fireplace across the room from them. Not that it would help since the fire had been long ago extinguished.

He refused to let the sale of the *ristorante*— the deal he'd been negotiating for weeks—go up in smoke because of some promotional deal his grandfather had signed. There had to be a way around it. Dante wondered how much it'd take to convince Lizzie to quietly return to New York.

"I'm sure we can reach some sort of agreement." He was, after all, a DeFiore. He had access to a sizable fortune. "What will it take for you to forget about your arrangement with my grandfather?"

She sat up straighter. "Nothing."

"What do you mean nothing?"

"I mean that I'm not leaving." She leaned forward, pressing her elbows down on the tabletop. "I don't think you understand how serious I am. I've cut out months of my life for this internship. I've said goodbye to my family and friends in order to be here. I had to quit my job. Are you getting the picture? Everything is riding on this agreement—my entire future. I have a signed agreement and I intend to film a television segment in that kitchen." She pointed over her shoulder.

She'd quit her job!

Who did something like that? Obviously someone very trusting or very desperate. Which type was she? Her beautiful face showed lines of stress and the darkness below her eyes hinted at her exhaustion. He was leaning toward the desperate scenario.

Perhaps he'd been too rough on her. He really hadn't meant to upset her. He knew how frustrating it could be to be so close to getting what you wanted and yet having a barricade thrown in the way.

"Listen, I know this isn't what you want to hear, but I'm sure you'll be able to land another job somewhere else—"

"And what are you planning to do about the film crew when they arrive?"

Dante's lips pressed together. Yes, what was he going to do? This situation was getting ever so complicated. He eyed up the woman. Was she on the level? Was she truly after the work experience? The opportunity to learn? Or was she an opportunist playing on his sympathies?

He certainly didn't want to spend his time inflating her ego in front of the camera crew for the next two months—two very long months. But he was getting the very unsettling feeling that there was no way over, around or under the arrangement without a lengthy, messy lawsuit, which would hold up the sale of the *ristorante*.

This was not how things were supposed to go.

Lizzie resisted the urge to get up and start pacing. It was what she usually did when she was stuck in a tough spot. While growing up in the foster care system, she'd found herself in plenty of tough spots. But the one thing she'd learned through it all was not to give up—if it was important enough, there had to be a solution. It'd worked to keep Jules, her foster sister, with her through the years. She just had to take a deep breath and not panic.

Dante appeared to be a businessman. Surely he'd listen to logic. It was her last alternative. She sucked in a steadying breath, willing her mind to calm. "If you'll read over the contract, you'll see that your grandfather has agreed not only to mentor me but also to host a television crew. We're doing a reality spot for one of the cooking shows. It's been in the works for months now. Your grandfather was very excited about the project and how it'd give this place—" she waved her hand around at the restaurant that had a very distinct air about it "—international recognition. Just think of all the people that would know the name Ristorante Massimo."

Dante's eyes lit up with interest. "Do you have some numbers to back up your claims?"

She would have brought them, if she'd known she'd need them. "Your grandfather is confident in the value of these television segments. He has made numerous appearances on the culinary channel and has made quite a name for himself."

"I know. I was here for every one of those appearances."

She studied Dante's face for some recollection of him. His tanned skin. His dark eyes. His strong jaw. And those lips… Oh, they looked good enough to kiss into submission… She jerked her attention back to the conversation. "Why don't I recall seeing you in any of them?"

"Because I took a very small role in them. I didn't understand why my grandfather would sign up for those television appearances."

Her gaze narrowed in on him. "Do you have something against people on television?"

"No." He crossed his arms and leaned back, rocking his chair on the rear two legs. "I just think in a lot of cases they misrepresent life. They give people false hope that they'll be overnight successes. Most of the time life doesn't work that way. Life is a lot harder."

There was a glimmer of something in his eyes. Was it regret? Or pain? In a blink, his feelings were once again hidden. She was locked out. And for some reason that bothered her. Not that it should—it wasn't as though they were friends. She didn't even know him.

Not about to waste her time debating the positive and negative points of television, she decided to turn the conversation back around to her reason for being here. "Surely your grandfather will be back soon. After all, he has a restaurant to run."

"I'm afraid that he won't be returning."

"He won't?" This was news to her. Surely he couldn't be right. "But we have an agreement. And he was so eager for us to begin."

Dante rubbed his jaw as though trying to decide if he should say more. His dark gaze studied her intently. It made her want to squirm in her seat but she resisted.

"Whatever you're thinking, just say it. I need to know what's going on."

Dante sighed. "My grandfather recently experienced a stroke. He has since moved to the country."

"Oh, no." She pressed a hand to her chest. This was so much worse than she'd imagined. "Is he going to be all right?"

Dante's brows lifted as though he was surprised by her concern. "Yes, it wasn't as bad as it could have been. He's getting therapy."

"Thank goodness. Your grandfather seemed so lively and active. I just can't imagine that happening to him."

She thought back to their lively emails and chatty phone conversations. Massimo's voice had been rich and robust like a dark roast espresso. He was what she thought of when she imagined having a grandfather of her own. "He was so full of life."

"How exactly did you get to know him?"

Perhaps she'd said too much. It wasn't as if she and Massimo were *that* close. "At first, the production group put us in touch. We emailed back and forth. Then we started talking on the phone, discussing how we wanted to handle the time slots. After all, they are short, so we couldn't get too elaborate. But then again, we didn't want to skimp and do just the basics."

"Sounds like you two talked quite a bit."

She shrugged. "It wasn't like we talked every day. More like when one of us had a good idea. But that was hampered by the time difference. And then recently the calls stopped. When I phoned here I was merely told that he wasn't available and that they'd give him a message."

Dante's eyes opened wide as though a thought had come to him. "I remember seeing those messages. I had no idea who you were or what you wanted. I was beginning to wonder if my grand-father had a girlfriend on the side."

"Nope, it was me. And now that you know the whole story, what's yours?"

"My what?"

"Story. I take it you run this place for your grandfather."

His brows furrowed together as though he knew where this conversation was leading. "Yes, I do."

"Have you worked here long?" She wanted as much information as possible so she could plot out a backup plan.

He hesitantly nodded.

"That must be wonderful to learn from such a talented chef." There had to be a way to salvage this deal. But she needed to know more. "When did you start working with your grandfather?"

"When I was a kid, I would come and visit. But it wasn't until later that I worked here full-time."

She noticed that his answers were vague at best, giving her no clue as to his family life or why he came here to work. Perhaps he needed the money. Still, as she stared across the table at him, his whole demeanor spoke of money and culture. She also couldn't dismiss the fact that most women would find him alarmingly handsome. In fact, he'd make some real eye candy for the television spot. And if that was what it took to draw in an audience, who was she to argue.

She'd been earning money cooking since she was fourteen. Of course, being so young, she'd been paid under the table. Over the years, she'd gained more and more experience, but never thinking she'd ever have a shot at owning a restaurant of her own, she'd taken the safe route and gone to college. She'd needed a way to make decent money to keep herself and Jules afloat.

But then Jules entered her application for a reality TV cooking show. Jules had insisted that she needed to take a risk and follow her dream of being a chef in her own five-star restaurant.

Winning that reality show had been a huge stepping-stone. It gave her a television contract and a plane ticket to Rome, where she'd learn from the best in the business. Jules was right. Maybe her dream would come true.

All she needed was to make sure this deal was a success. One way or the other. And if Chef Massimo couldn't participate then perhaps his grandson would do.

She eyed him up. "Your grandfather must have taught you all of his secrets in the kitchen."

His body noticeably stiffened. "Yes, he did. How else would I keep the place running in his absence?"

She knew it was akin to poking a sleeping bear with a stick, but she had to confirm her suspicions before she altered her plans ever so slightly. "But do your dishes taste like your grandfather's?"

"The customers don't know the difference." The indignity in his voice rumbled through the room. "Who do you think took the time to learn every tiny detail of my grandfather's recipes? My grandfather insisted that if you were going to do something, you should learn to do it right. And there were no shortcuts in his kitchen."

From the little she'd known of Massimo, she could easily believe this was true. During their phone conversations, he'd made it clear that he didn't take shortcuts with his recipes or with training people. She'd have to start from the beginning. Normally, she'd have taken it as an insult, but coming from Massimo, she had the feeling that he only wanted the best for both of them and the television spotlight.

"Will you continue to run the restaurant alone?"

Dante ran a hand over his jaw. "Are you always this curious about strangers?"

She wasn't about to back off. This information was important and she had learned almost everything she needed. "I'm just trying to make a little conversation. Is that so wrong?"

There was a look in his eyes that said he didn't believe her. Still, he didn't press the subject. Instead he surprised her by answering. "For the foreseeable future I will continue to run Massimo's. I can't predict the future."

"I still wonder if you're as good as your grandfather in the kitchen."

"Wait here." He jumped to his feet and strode out of the room.

Where in the world had he gone? She was tempted to follow, but she thought better of it. She'd already pushed her luck as far as she dared. But her new plan was definitely taking shape.

The only problem she envisioned was trying to keep her mind on the art of cooking and not on the hottie mentoring her. She knew jet lag was to blame for her distorted worries. A little uninterrupted sleep would have her thinking clearly.

This arrangement was far too important to ruin due to some sort of crush. She pursed her lips together. No matter how good he looked, she knew better than to let her heart rule her mind. She knew too well the agonizing pain of rejection and abandonment. She wouldn't subject herself to that again. Not for anyone.

She pulled her shoulders back and clasped her hands in her lap. Time to put her plan in motion.

One way or the other.

CHAPTER THREE

HOW DARE SHE question his prowess in the kitchen?

Dante stared down at a plate of *pasta alla gricia*, one of his favorite dishes. The fine balance of cured pork and *pecorino romano* gave the pasta a unique, tangy flavor. It was a dish he never grew tired of eating.

He proceeded to divvy the food between two plates. After all, he didn't need that much to eat at this late hour. As he arranged the plates, he wondered why he was going to such bother. What was so special about this golden-haired beauty? And why did he feel a compulsion to prove himself where she was concerned?

It wasn't as if he was ever going to see Lizzie again. Without his grandfather around to hold up his end of the agreement, she'd be catching the next plane back to New York. Still, before she left, he needed to prove his point. He'd taken some of his grandfather's recipes and put his own twist on them. And the patrons loved them. This meal was sure not to disappoint the most discerning palate.

He strode back into the dining room and placed a plate in front of Lizzie. She gazed up at him with a wide-eyed blue gaze. Her mouth gaped as though she were about to say something, but no words came out.

He stared at her lush lips, painted with a shimmery pink frost. They looked perfectly ripe for a kiss. The urge grew stronger with each passing second. The breath hitched in his throat.

"This looks delicious." She was staring at him, not the food. And she was smiling.

"It's an old family recipe." He nearly tripped over his own feet as he moved to the other side of the table. "The secret to the dish is to keep it simple and not be tempted to add extras. You don't want to detract from the flavor of the meat and cheese."

He couldn't believe he was letting her good looks and charms get to him. It wasn't as if she was the first beautiful woman he'd entertained. But she was the first that he truly wanted to impress. Safely in his seat, he noticed the smallness of the table. If he wasn't careful, his legs would brush against hers. If this were a casual date, he'd take advantage of the coziness, but Lizzie was different from the usual women he dated. She was more serious. More intent. And she seemed to have only one thing on her mind—business.

"Aren't you going to try it?" Dante motioned to the food. Just because he wasn't interested in helping her with her dreams of stardom didn't mean he couldn't prove his point—he could create magic in the kitchen.

He watched as she spun the pasta on her fork and slipped it in her mouth. He sat there captivated, waiting for her reaction. When she moaned her approval, his blood pressure spiked and his grip tightened on the fork.

"This is very good. Did you make it?"

Her question didn't fool him. He knew what she was digging at—she wanted him to step up and fill in for his grandfather. Him on television— never. That was his grandfather's dream—not his.

"It's delicious." She flashed him a big smile, seemingly unfazed by his tight-lipped expression.

Her smile gave him a strange feeling in his chest that shoved him off center. And that wasn't good. He didn't want to be vulnerable to a woman. He knew for a fact that romance would ultimately lead to disaster—one way or the other.

He forced himself to eat because he hadn't had time to since that morning and his body must be starved. But he didn't really have an appetite. In fact, the food tasted like cardboard. Thankfully Lizzie seemed impressed with it.

When she'd cleaned her plate, she pushed it aside. "Thank you. I can't wait for you to teach me how to make it."

Dante still had a couple of bites left on his plate when he set his fork down and moved the plate aside. "That isn't going to happen."

"Maybe you should at least consider it."

Her gaze strayed to the contract that was still sitting in the middle of the table and then back to him. What was she implying? That she'd drag him through the courts?

That was the last thing he needed. He already had enough important issues on his mind, including fixing his relationship with his family. And the closer it got to putting his signature on the sale papers, the more unsettled he'd become about his decision.

"You can't expect me to fulfill my grandfather's agreement."

"Why not?" She smiled as though it would melt

his resistance. Maybe under different circumstances it would have worked, but not now.

"Because I don't want to be on television. I didn't like it when those camera people were here before. All they did was get in the way and create a circus of onlookers wanting to get their faces on television."

He didn't bother to mention that he was just days away from closing a deal to sell Ristorante Massimo. But it all hinged on those family recipes. And somehow parting with those felt treasonous. His grandfather had signed the entire business over to him to do as he pleased, but still he couldn't make this caliber of decision on his own.

But how did he approach his grandfather? How did he tell him that he felt restless again and without Massimo in the kitchen, it just wasn't the same? It was time he moved on to find something that pacified the uneasiness in him.

He'd been toying with the thought of returning to the vineyard and working alongside his father and brother. After all of this time, perhaps he and his father could call a truce—perhaps Dante could in some small way try to make up for the loss and unhappiness his father had endured in the years since Dante's mother had died. But was that even possible considering their strained relationship?

"It isn't me you have to worry about." Lizzie's voice drew him back to the here and now. She toyed with the cloth napkin. "The television people will want to enforce the contract. They're already advertising the segment on their station. I saw it before I left New York. Granted, we won't have a show of our own. But we will have a daily spot on the most popular show on their station."

He'd forgotten that there was a third party to this agreement. A television conglomerate would not be easily deterred from enforcing their rights. "But what makes you think that they would want me instead of my grandfather?"

"I take it your grandfather truly didn't mention any of this to you?"

Dante shook his head. A sick feeling churned in the pit of his stomach.

"That's strange. When he brought your name up to the television people, I thought for sure he'd discussed it with you." She shrugged. "Anyway, they are eager to have you included in the segments. They think you'll appeal to the younger viewers."

Dante leaned his head back and expelled a

weary sigh. Why hadn't his grandfather mentioned any of this to him? Maybe Massimo just never got the chance. Regardless, this situation was going from bad to worse. What was next?

When Dante didn't say anything, Lizzie continued, "I'm sure when I explain to them about your grandfather no longer being able to fulfill his role, they will welcome a young, handsome replacement."

She thought he was handsome? He sat up a little straighter. "And if I don't agree—"

"From what I read, there are monetary penalties for not fulfilling the contract. I'm not an attorney but you might want to have someone take a look at it."

A court battle would only extend the time it would take to sell the *ristorante*. Not to mention scare off his potential buyer—the one with deep pockets and an interest in keeping Ristorante Massimo as is.

Dante's gaze moved to the document. "Do you mind if I keep these papers for a little while?"

"That's fine. It's a copy."

"I'll get back to you on this." He got to his feet. He had a lot to think over. It was time to call it a night.

"You'll have to decide soon, as the film crew will be here in a couple of days."

His back teeth ground together. Talk about finding everything out at the last minute. No matter his decision, resolving this issue would take some time. Agreeing to the filming would be much quicker than a court suit. And in the end, would he win the lawsuit?

But then again, could he work with Lizzie for two months and ignore the way her smile made his pulse race? Or the way her eyes drew him in? What could he say? He was a red-hot Italian man who appreciated women. But nothing about Lizzie hinted at her being open to a casual, gratifying experience. And he was not about to get tangled up in something that involved his heart. Nothing could convince him to risk it—not after the carnage he'd witnessed. No way.

He was attracted to her.

Lizzie secretly reveled in the knowledge. Not that either of them would act on it. She'd noticed how he kept his distance, but his eyes betrayed him. She wondered if his demeanor had cooled because of the television show. Or was there something more? Her gaze slipped to his hands, not spying any rings. Still, that didn't mean there wasn't a significant other.

Realizing the implication of what she was doing, she jerked her gaze upward. But that wasn't any better as she ended up staring into his bottomless eyes. Her heart thudded against her ribs. This was not good. Not good at all.

She glanced down at the gleaming black-and-white floor tiles. She could still feel him staring at her. With great effort, she ignored him. Her trip to Rome was meant to be a learning experience, not to partake in a holiday romance.

Putting herself out there and getting involved with Dante was foolish. She had the scars on her heart to prove that romance could come with a high price tag. Besides, she was certain she wouldn't live up to his expectations—she never did.

It was much easier to wear a smile and keep people at arm's length. It was safer. And that was exactly how she planned to handle this situation.

Dante cleared his throat. "Well, since you're a couple of days early, I'm sure you'll want to tour the city. There's lots to see and experience." He led her to the front door. "Make sure you visit the Colosseum and the catacombs."

"I'm looking forward to sightseeing. This is my first trip to Italy. Actually, it's my first trip anywhere." She pressed her lips together to keep from spilling details of her pitiful life. She didn't want his sympathy. She was just so excited about this once-in-a-lifetime experience. Years ago in those foster homes, she never would have imagined that a trip like this would be a possibility—let alone a reality.

"I'd start with the Vatican Museums."

"Thanks. I will."

He smiled as he pulled open the door. The tired lines on his face smoothed and his eyes warmed. She was struck by how truly handsome he was when he let his guard down. She'd have to be careful and not fall for this mysterious Italian.

She glanced out into the dark night. "Is this the way to the apartment?"

His brow puckered. "Excuse me."

"The apartment. Massimo told me that he had a place for me to stay?"

"He did?" Dante uttered the words as though they were part of his thought process and not a question for her.

She nodded and reached into her purse. She fumbled around until her fingers stumbled across some folded papers. Her fingers clasped them and pulled them out.

"I have the email correspondence." She held out the evidence. "It's all right here."

Dante waved away the pages. "Are you this prepared for everything?"

She nodded. She'd learned a long time ago that people rarely keep their word. Just like her mother, who'd promised she'd do whatever it took to get Lizzie back from social services. In the beginning, Lizzie had gone to bed each night crying for the only parent she'd ever known—the mother who was big on neglect and sparing on kindness. At the time, Lizzie hadn't known any other way. In the end, that mother-daughter reunion was not to be. Her mother had been all talk and no follow-through, unable to move past the drugs and alcohol. Lizzie languished in the system.

She'd grown up knowing one simple truth: people rarely lived up to their word. There was only one person to count on—herself.

However, in Massimo's case, breaking his word was totally understandable. It was beyond his control. Her heart squeezed when she thought of that outgoing man being forced into retirement. She truly hoped while she was here that she'd get the opportunity to meet him and thank him for having such faith in her. It was as though he could see through her brave front to her quivering insides. During moments of doubt, he'd calmed her and assured her that all would be fine with the television segments.

She glanced at Dante. He definitely wasn't a calming force like his grandfather. If anything, Dante's presence filled her with nervous energy.

He leaned against the door. "There's no apartment available."

Her eyes narrowed on him. "Does everything with you have to be a struggle?"

"I'm not trying to be difficult. I simply don't have any place for you to stay."

"Why is it your grandfather seemed confident that I would be comfortable here?"

"Probably because there was a remodeled apartment available, but since I wasn't privy to your arrangement with my grandfather, I just leased it. But I'm sure you won't have a problem finding a hotel room nearby."

Oh, yes, there would be a big problem. She didn't have money to rent a hotel room. She could only imagine how expensive that would be and she needed every penny to pay down her debts and to pay tuition for Jules's grad school. Every penny from the contract was already accounted for. There was nothing to spare.

"It was agreed that I would have free room and board." Pride dictated that she keep it to herself that she didn't have the money to get a hotel room.

He crossed his arms and stared at her as though debating his options. "What do you want me to do? Give you my bed?"

The words sparked a rush of tempting images to dance through her mind. Dante leaning in and pressing his very tempting lips to hers. His long, lean fingers grazing her cheek before resting against the beating pulse in her throat. Her leaning into him as he swept her up in his arms.

"Lizzie, are you okay?" Dante's eyes filled with concern.

She swallowed hard, realizing that she'd let her imagination get the best of her. "Umm, yes. I'm just a little jet-lagged. And things were busy tonight, keeping me on my toes."

His eyes probed her. "Are you sure that's all it is?"

She nodded.

Where in the world had those distracting images of Dante come from? It wasn't as though she was looking for a boyfriend. The last man in her life had believed they should each have their own space until one day he dropped by to let her know that he was moving to California to chase his dream of acting. No *I'll miss you.* Or *Will you come with me?*

He'd tossed her aside like the old worn-out couch and the back issues of his rocker magazines. He hadn't wanted her except for a little fun here and there. She'd foolishly let herself believe that they were building something special. In the end, she hadn't been enough for him—she always came up lacking.

"I'd really like to get some rest." And some distance from Dante so she could think clearly. "It's been a long evening and my feet are killing me."

Was that a hint of color rising in his cheeks? Did he feel bad about putting her to work? Maybe he should, but she honestly didn't mind. She liked meeting some of the people she'd hopefully be cooking for in the near future. That was if she ever convinced Dante that this arrangement could work.

"Putting you to work was a total mix-up. My

apologies." He glanced down at the floor. "I owe you."

"Apology accepted." She loved that he had manners. "Now, does this mean you'll find me a bed?"

CHAPTER FOUR

THE QUESTION CONJURED up all sorts of scintillating scenarios.

Dante squelched his overactive, overeager imagination. Something told him that there was a whole lot more to this beautiful woman than her desire to be on television and to brush up on her skills in the kitchen. He saw in her eyes a guardedness. He recognized the look because it was something he'd witnessed with his older brother after his young wife had tragically died. It was a look one got when life had double-crossed them.

Lizzie had traveled to the other side of the globe from her home without knowing a single soul, and from the determined set of her mouth, she wasn't about to turn tail and run. She was willing to stand her ground. And he couldn't help but admire her strength.

He just hoped his gut feeling about this woman wasn't off target. What he had in mind was a bold move. But his grandfather, who'd always been a good judge of character, liked her. He surely wouldn't have gone out of his way for her if he hadn't. But that didn't mean Dante should trust her completely, especially when it came to his grandfather.

Nonno had enough on his plate. Since he'd been struck down by a stroke, he'd been lost in a sea of self-pity. Dante was getting desperate to snap his grandfather back into the world of the living. And plying the man with problems when Nonno was already down wouldn't help anyone.

"Have you told me everything now? About your agreement with my grandfather."

She nodded.

"You promise? No more surprises?"

"Cross my heart." Her finger slowly crossed her chest.

Dante cleared his throat as he forced his gaze upward to meet her eyes. "I suppose I do have a place for you to stay."

"Lead the way."

With the main doors locked, he moved next to her on the sidewalk. "It's right over here."

He led the way to a plain red door alongside the restaurant. With a key card, the door buzzed and he pulled it open for her. Inside was a small but lush lobby with an elevator and a door leading to steps. He'd made sure to give the building a face-lift when his grandfather handed over the reins to him. That was all it took to draw in eager candidates to rent the one available unit that he'd been occupying until he'd moved into his grandfather's much larger apartment.

"Where are we going?" She glanced around at the new furnishings adorning the lobby.

"There are apartments over the *ristorante*."

A look of dawning glinted in her eyes. "Your grandfather mentioned those. It's where he intended for me to stay while I am here. Are they nice?"

"Quite nice." In fact the renovations on his apartment had just been completed.

As the elevator doors slid open, she paused and turned to him. "But I thought you said that you leased the last one."

"Do you want to see what I have in mind or not?"

She nodded before stepping inside the elevator.

Good. Because he certainly wasn't going to bend over backward to make her happy. In fact, if she walked away now of her own accord, so much the better. As it was, this arrangement would be only temporary. He'd pacify her until he spoke to his solicitor.

In the cozy confines of the elevator, the faint scent of her floral perfume wrapped around him and teased his senses. If she were anyone else, he'd comment on its intoxicating scent. It was so tempting to lean closer and draw the perfume deeper into his lungs. But he resisted. Something about her led him to believe that she'd want more than one night—more than he was capable of offering her.

The thought of letting go and falling in love made his gut tighten and his palms grow damp. He'd witnessed firsthand the power of love and it wasn't all sappy ballads and roses. Love had the strength to crush a person, leaving them broken and angry at the world.

He placed a key in the pad, turned it and pressed the penthouse button. The hum of the elevator was the only sound. In no time at all the door swished open, revealing a red-carpeted hallway. He led her to his door, adorned with gold emblems that read PH-1.

Dante unlocked the door and waved for her to go ahead of him. He couldn't help but watch her face. She definitely wouldn't make much of a poker player as her emotions filtered across her face. Her blue eyes opened wide as she took in the pillar posts that supported the open floor plan for the living room and kitchen area.

He'd had walls torn down in order to create this spacious area. He may enjoy city life but the country boy in him didn't like to feel completely hemmed in. He'd paid the men bonuses to turn the renovations around quickly. Though it didn't come close in size to his family's home at the vineyard, the apartment was still large—large enough for two people to coexist without stepping on each other's toes. At least for one night.

She walked farther into the room. She paused next to the black leather couch and turned to him. "Do you live here alone?"

"I do. My grandfather used to live here. When he got sick, he turned it over to me. I made some changes and had everything updated."

"It certainly is spacious. I think I'd get lost in a place this size." Her stiff posture said that she was as uncomfortable as he felt.

He wasn't used to having company. He'd been so busy since his grandfather's sudden exit from the *ristorante*—from his life—that he didn't have time for a social life. In fact, now that he thought about it, Lizzie was the first woman he'd had in here. He wasn't sure how he felt about that fact.

"Can I get you anything?" he asked, trying to ease the mounting discomfort.

"Yes—you can tell me what I'm doing here."

Oh, yes. He thought it was obvious but apparently it wasn't to her. "You can stay here tonight until we can get this whole situation cleared up."

"You mean when you consent to the contents of this contract."

His jaw tightened, holding back a string of heated words.

"Don't look like it's the end of the world." Lizzie stepped up to him. "With your good looks, the camera is going to love you. And that's not to mention the thousands of women watching the segment. Who knows, maybe you'll become a star."

Dante laughed. Him a star. Never. Her lush lips lifted. The simple expression made her eyes sparkle like blue topaz. Her pale face filled with color. And her lips, they were plump and just right to lean in and snag a sweet taste. His head started to lower when she pulled back as though reading his errant thoughts.

He cleared his throat and moved to the kitchenette to retrieve a glass. "Are you sure you don't want anything to drink?"

"I'm fine. Have you lived here long?"

He ran the water until it was cold—real cold. What he really needed to do was dump it over his head and shock some sense back into himself.

"I've lived in this building since I moved to Rome. I had a smaller apartment on another floor before moving to this one. You're my first guest here." He turned, waiting to hear more about what she thought of the place. "What do you think of it?"

He was genuinely curious about her take on the place. It was modeled in black-and-white decor. With the two colors, it made decorating easier for him. He sensed that it still needed something, but he couldn't put his finger on what exactly was missing.

"It's…it's nice." Her tone was hesitant.

Nice? The muscles in his neck tightened. Who said "nice"? Someone who was trying to be polite when they really didn't like something but they didn't want to hurt the other person's feelings.

She leaned back on the couch and straightened her legs. She lifted her arms over her head and stretched. He tried to ignore how her blouse rode up and exposed a hint of her creamy skin. But it was too late. His thoughts strayed in the wrong direction again. At this rate, he'd need a very cold shower.

He turned his attention back to the apartment and glanced around, trying to see it from her perspective. Everything was new. There wasn't a speck of dust—his cleaning lady had just been there. And he made sure to always pick up after himself. There wasn't a stray sock to be had anywhere.

"Is it the black-and-white decor you don't like?" He really wanted to know. Maybe her answer would shed some light on why he felt something was off about the place.

"I told you, I like it."

"But describing it as *nice* is what people say to be polite. I want to know what's missing." There, he'd said it. There was something missing and it was going to drive him crazy until he figured it out.

He looked around at the white walls. The modern artwork. The two pieces of sculpture. One of a stallion rearing up. The other of a gentle mare. They reminded him of home. When he turned around, he noticed Lizzie unzipping her boots and easing them off. Her pink-painted toes stretched and then pointed as though she were a ballerina as she worked out all of the muscles. When she murmured her pleasure at being free of the boots, he thought he was going to lose it. It took every bit of willpower to remain in his spot and not go to her.

He turned his back. He tried to think of something to do. Something to keep him from going to her. But there was nothing that needed straightening up. No dirty dishes in the sink. In fact, he spent very little time here. For the most part, he slept here and that was it. The rest of his time was spent either downstairs in the *ristorante* or at the vineyard, checking on his grandfather.

"You know what's missing?" Her voice drew his attention.

He turned around and tried to ignore the way her short black skirt had ridden even higher on her thighs. "What would that be?"

"There are no pictures. I thought there'd be one of you with your grandfather."

Dante glanced around, realizing she was right. He didn't have a single picture of anyone. "I'm sorry. I don't have any pictures here. They are all at my family's home."

"Do they live far from here?"

He shrugged. "It's a bit of a drive. But not that far. I like to go home on the weekends."

"But isn't the restaurant open?"

"It's open Saturday. But then we're closed Sunday and Monday. So my weekend is not the traditional weekend."

"I see. And your grandfather, is he with your family?"

Dante nodded. "He lives with my father and older brother."

Her brows drew together but she didn't say anything. He couldn't help but be curious about her thoughts. Everything about this woman poked at his curiosity.

"What are you wondering?"

She shook her head. "Nothing."

"Go ahead. Say what's on your mind."

"You mentioned a lot of men. Are there no women?"

"Afraid not. Unless you count my aunts, but they don't live there even though they are around so much that it feels like they do." He didn't want to offer a detailed explanation of why there were no women living at the vineyard. He tried to avoid that subject at all costs. He took it for granted that the DeFiore men were to grow old alone. But that was a subject best left for another day.

"Sounds like you have a big family."

"That's the understatement of the century." Anxious to end this line of conversation, he said, "We should get some sleep. Tomorrow will be here before we know it."

"You're sure you want me to stay here?" She stared directly at him.

Their gazes connected and held. Beyond the beauty of her eyes, there was something more that drew him to her—a vulnerability. In that moment, he longed to ride to her rescue and sweep her into his arms. He'd hold her close and kiss away her worries.

Lizzie glanced away, breaking the special moment.

Was she thinking the same thing as him? Did she feel the pull of attraction, too? Not that he was going to act on his thoughts. It wasn't as though he couldn't keep himself in check. He could and would be a gentleman.

"I'll deal with it. After all, you said this is what my grandfather agreed to. There are a couple of guest rooms down the hallway." He pointed to the right. And then for good measure he added, "And the master suite is in that direction." His hand gestured to the left. "Plenty of room for both of us."

"My luggage hasn't arrived yet. I have nothing to sleep in."

"I can loan you something."

Just as he said that, there was a buzz from the intercom. He went to answer it. In seconds, he returned to her. "Well, you don't have to worry. Your luggage has arrived."

She smiled. "That's great."

A moment of disappointment coursed through him. What in the world was the matter with him? Why should he care one way or the other if she slept in one of his shirts or not? Obviously he was more tired than he'd thought.

CHAPTER FIVE

LIZZIE GRINNED AND STRETCHED, like a cat that had spent the afternoon napping in the sunshine. She glanced around the unfamiliar surroundings, noticing the sun's rays creeping past the white sheers over the window. She rubbed her eyes and then fumbled for her cell phone. She was shocked to find that she'd slept away half of the morning. It was going to take her a bit to get her internal alarm clock reset.

Last night, she'd been so tired that she'd barely gotten off a text message to Jules to assure her that she'd arrived safely before sleep claimed her. This was the first time in their lives that they'd been separated for an extended period and Lizzie already missed her foster sister, who was also her best friend. She had promised to call today to fill her in on her trip. But after converting the time, Lizzie realized it was too early in New York to call.

She glanced around, not surprised to find the

room done up in black and white. The man may be drop-dead gorgeous but when it came to decorating, he definitely lacked imaginative skills. What this place needed was some warmth—a woman's touch.

She thought back to his comment about her being his first guest here. She found that surprising. For some reason, she imagined someone as sexy and charming as him having a woman on each arm. Perhaps there was more to this man than his smooth talk and devastating smile. What was the real Dante like? Laid-back and flirtatious? Serious and a workaholic?

She paused and listened for any sounds from him. But then again, with an apartment this big, she doubted she'd hear him in the kitchen. She'd be willing to bet that her entire New York apartment could fit in this bedroom. She'd never been in such a spacious home before. Not that she'd have time to get used to it. She was pretty certain that Dante was only mollifying her. Today he would have a plan to get her out of his life and his restaurant.

With that thought in mind, Lizzie sprang out of bed and rushed into the glass block shower enclosure with more water jets than she'd ever imagined were possible. But instead of enjoying the shower, she wondered what Dante's next move would be concerning the agreement.

Almost thirty minutes later, her straight blond hair was smoothed back into the normal ponytail that she wore due to its ease at pinning it up in the kitchen. She slipped on a dark pair of designer jeans. Lizzie didn't recognize the name, but the lady at the secondhand store had assured her that they were the in thing right now.

Lizzie pulled on a white tiny tee with sparkly silver bling on the front in the shape of a smiley face. It was fun, and today she figured she just might need something uplifting. There were decisions to be made.

After she stepped into a pair of black cotton shoes, she soundlessly made her way to the living room, finding it deserted. Where could Dante be? She recalled their conversation last night and she was certain that he'd said the restaurant was closed today.

"Dante?" Nothing. "Dante?" she called out, louder this time.

Suddenly he was standing in the hallway that led to the master suite. "Sorry, I didn't hear you. Have you been up long?"

She shook her head. "I'm afraid that my body is still on New York time."

"I've spoken to my grandfather."

Lizzie's chest tightened. "What did he say?"

Dante paused, making her anxiety even worse. She wanted to yell at him to spit it out. Did Massimo say something that was going to change how this whole scenario played out?

"He didn't say much. I'm getting ready to go see him."

She waited, hoping Dante would extend an invitation. When he didn't, she added, "How far did you say the vineyard is from here?"

He shrugged. "An hour or so out of the city."

She glanced toward the elongated window. "It's a beautiful day for a drive."

He said nothing.

Why wasn't he taking the hint? If she laid it on any thicker, she'd have to invite herself along. She resisted the urge to stamp her feet in frustration. Why wouldn't he give in and offer her a ride? She'd already mentioned how much she enjoyed talking to his grandfather on the phone.

Maybe Dante just wasn't good with hints, no matter how bold they were. Perhaps she should try another approach—a direct one.

"I'd like to meet your grandfather."

Dante shook his head. "That isn't going to happen."

Oh, no. She wasn't giving up that easily. "Why not? When we talked on the phone, he was very excited about my arrival."

"Things have changed since then." Dante walked over and grabbed his keys from the edge of the kitchen counter. "It just wouldn't be a good idea."

"Did you even tell him that I was here?"

Dante's gaze lowered. "In passing."

He was leaving something out but what? "And did you discuss the contract?"

"No. He had a bad night and he was agitated this morning. I didn't think him hearing about what has transpired since your arrival would help things." He cursed under his breath and strode over to the door and grabbed his overnight bag.

He was leaving without her.

Disappointment washed over her. She just couldn't shake her desire to meet the man who reminded her of what she imagined her grandfathers would have been like, if she'd ever met either of her own. But she couldn't tell Dante that.

He'd think she was a sentimental dreamer—and she couldn't blame him.

How could she ever explain to someone who grew up in a big, caring family with parents and grandparents about the gaping hole in her heart? She'd forever been on the outside looking in. She knew all too well that families weren't perfect. Her friends in school had dealt with a whole host of family dynamics, but they had a common element—love to bind them together, no matter what. And to have her very own family was what Lizzie had prayed for each night. And at Christmastime it had been the only thing she had ever asked for from Santa.

Instead of a mom and dad and grandparents, she was given Jules—her foster sister. And she loved her with all of her heart. She would do anything for her, including keeping her promise to help Jules reach for her dreams—no matter the price. Because of their dismal finances, Jules had to put off college for a couple of years until Lizzie got her degree. Jules always talked of helping other kids like them. This was Jules's chance to become a social worker and make a difference, but in order to do that she had to get through grad school first.

Massimo had been insistent that her plan would work. He'd been so certain. And she couldn't shake her desire to meet him and thank him for his encouragement. "Take me with you. I promise I won't say or do anything to upset your grand-father."

Dante eyed her up as though attempting to gauge her sincerity. She sent him a pleading look. Under the intensity of his stare, her insides quiv-ered. But she refused to turn away.

"Even though he insists on meeting you, I will leave you behind if I feel I can't trust you."

"So he does want to meet me." This time she did smile.

"Don't go getting all excited. I still haven't made up my mind about taking you with me. You know it's a bit of a ride."

Meaning Dante didn't like the thought of spend-ing yet more time alone with her. To be honest, she couldn't blame him. She'd basically dropped into his life out of nowhere with absolutely no warning. How could she possibly expect him to react any different?

But then again, she had noticed the way he'd looked at her last night. As if she were an ice cream cone on a sweltering hot day and he couldn't wait to lick her up. To be fair, she'd had similar thoughts about him. No one had ever turned her on with just a look.

She halted her thoughts. It wasn't worth it to go down this path. It'd only lead to heartbreak—her heartbreak. In her experience, men only wanted an uncomplicated good time. And she couldn't separate her heart and her mind. It was so much easier to remain detached. If she was smart, she'd turn and leave now. But she couldn't. Not yet.

"You can trust me," she pleaded. "I won't upset Massimo."

"I don't know—"

"If you won't take me to him, then give me his address. I'll find my own way there."

Not that she had any clue how she'd get from point A to point B without a vehicle, but she was certain that Italy had public transportation. That was one of the things she'd discovered when she'd researched coming here. So now Dante wouldn't stand between her and meeting Massimo.

Dante hated being put in this position.

All he wanted to do was protect his grand-father—well, that wasn't quite the whole truth. He didn't relish the car ride with Lizzie. He was certain she'd keep at him, trying to convince him to change his mind about the television spot. His jaw tightened. He had other priorities with the sale of the *ristorante* to negotiate.

Then this morning when he'd phoned his grandfather to verify that he'd agreed to this television segment, his grandfather had come to life at the mention of Lizzie's name. After weeks of Nonno being in a black mood, this was the first time he'd sounded even remotely like himself. Dante made every excuse to get out of taking Lizzie to meet him. His grandfather would have none of it.

Unwilling to disappoint his grandfather, he said, "You can come with me on one stipulation."

Hope glinted in her eyes. "Name it."

"There will be no talking about the contract or the cooking show this weekend."

"But the camera crew will be here Tuesday morning expecting to begin filming before the restaurant opens. What will we do? We haven't even decided how to proceed."

"Let me deal with them." He'd already called his solicitor that morning. Even though it was the weekend, this couldn't wait. He'd pay the exorbitant fees. Whatever it took to find a way out of this mess.

She narrowed her gaze. "You're going to break the contract, aren't you?"

"Why wouldn't I? I never agreed to give up two months of my life."

"But I...I can't repay the money."

"What money?"

She glanced away and moved to the window that looked out over the street. "They paid me a portion of the fee up front. And it's already been spent. I can't repay them."

That wasn't his problem. But his conscience niggled at him. All in all, Lizzie wasn't bad. In fact, she was smokin' hot. And when she smiled it was as though a thousand-watt lightbulb had been switched on. But when she opened her mouth— well, that was a different story. She knew instinctively which buttons of his to push.

He wanted to think that she was lying to him just to gain his sympathy, but his gut was telling him that she was being truthful. Those unshed tears in her eyes—those were genuine. There had to be a compromise but he didn't know what that would be at this point.

Until he figured out what that was, he had to say something to ease her worry. "I can't promise you this will work out for you. But if you quit worrying while we're away, I give you my word that I'll share what my solicitor uncovers before I make any moves."

She hitched a slender hip and tilted her head to the side. He couldn't help but smile at the way she was eyeing him, trying to decide if she should trust him. He supposed he deserved it. He had just done the same thing to her.

The strained silence stretched on, making him uncomfortable. "Okay, you've made your point. I'll trust you not to pull the *poor pitiful me* card around my grandfather, if you'll trust me not to take any action without consulting you."

Why did he feel as if he'd just struck up a losing deal? For a man used to getting his way, this was a very unsettling feeling.

CHAPTER SIX

THIS WOULD IMPRESS HER.

Dante maneuvered his low-slung, freshly waxed, candy-apple-red sports car around the street corner and slowed to a crawl as he approached the front of the *ristorante*. Lizzie stood on the sidewalk with an overnight bag slung over her shoulder and her face lifted toward the sun. She didn't appear to notice him. The sun's rays gave her golden mane a shimmery glow. He wondered if she had any clue how her beauty commanded attention. Something told him she didn't. There was an unassuming air about her.

Without taking time to consider his actions, he tramped the brakes and reached for his smartphone to snap her picture. It wasn't until he returned it to the dash that he realized how foolish he was acting. Like some schoolkid with a crush on the most popular girl in school.

Back then he'd been so unsure of himself—not knowing how to act smooth around the girls. That all changed after he moved to Rome. Away from his father and brother, he'd grown more confident—more at ease with the ladies.

His older brother, though, always had a way with the women...but Stefano had eyes for only one girl, even back in school. They'd been childhood sweethearts until it came to a devastating end. The jarring memory brought Dante up short.

He eased the car forward and parked next to Lizzie. He jumped out and offered to take her bag, but she didn't release her hold. In fact, her grip tightened on the straps. What in the world?

"I just want to put it in the boot. There's no room inside the car. As you can see, it's rather compact."

She cast him a hesitant look before handing over the bag. He opened the door for her. Once she was seated, he stowed her bag with his. He was surprised how light she packed. He'd never met a woman who didn't need everything including the kitchen sink just to go away for the night. Lizzie was different in so many ways.

And now it was his chance to impress her with his pride and joy. Anytime he wanted to make a surefire impression on a woman, he pulled out Red. He'd bestowed the name upon the luxury sports car, not just because of its color but because the name implied an attitude, a fieriness, and that was how he felt when he was in the driver's seat.

"Ready?" He glanced at her as she perched a pair of dark sunglasses on her face, hiding her expressive eyes.

"Yes. I'm surprised you'd choose to drive."

"Why wouldn't I drive?" He revved the engine just because he could, and he loved how the motor roared with power.

Who complained about riding in a fine machine like this one? He'd dreamed about a powerful car like this all of his life, but his father made him wait—made him earn it on his own without dipping into his trust fund. At the time Dante had resented his father for standing in his way. Now Dante found himself grateful for the challenge. He'd learned an important lesson—he could accomplish whatever he set his mind to. Even his father had been impressed with the car, not that he'd said much, but Dante had seen it in his eyes the first time he'd driven up to the villa.

Lizzie adjusted her seat belt. "I thought I read somewhere that people utilize public transportation here."

He glanced at her as he slowed for a stop sign.

Was she serious? She'd prefer the train to his car? Impossible. "I thought the car would be more convenient. We can come and go as we need."

"Oh. Right. And do you always run stop signs?"

"What?"

"There was a stop sign back there. Didn't you see it?"

"Of course I did. Didn't you notice how I slowed down and checked that there was no cross traffic?"

"But you didn't stop."

His jaw tightened as he adjusted his grip on the steering wheel. "Are you always such a stickler for rules?"

"Yes. Is that a problem?"

"It depends."

Silence settled over them as Dante navigated them out of the city. Every now and then he sneaked a glance at Lizzie. She kept her face turned to the side. The tires clicked over the brick roadway as Rome passed by the window. The cars, the buildings and the people. He'd never been to New York City and he couldn't help but wonder if it was as beautiful as Rome. The lush green trees planted along stretches of roadway softened the view of block-and-mortar buildings. Thankfully it was Sunday, so the roadway wasn't congested with standstill traffic.

They quickly exited the city. Now was his chance to find out a little bit more about her before she met his grandfather. His gut told him there was a lot she was holding back. It was his duty to make sure there weren't any unpleasant surprises that might upset his grandfather. Dante assured himself that his interest was legitimate. It had absolutely nothing to do with unraveling the story behind the sad look in her eyes when she thought no one was watching her.

"Where in New York do you come from?"

Out of the corner of his eye he noticed how her head swung around quickly. "The Bronx. Why?"

"Just curious. I figured if we're going to be spending some time together, we might as well get to know a little about each other."

There was a poignant moment of silence as though she were deciding if this was a good idea or not. "And were you raised at this vineyard we're going to visit?"

Fair was fair. "Yes, I was. It's been in my family for generations. But it has grown over the years. And now our vino is a household name."

"That's an impressive legacy. So how did you

end up in Rome helping your grandfather run a restaurant?"

How in the world did this conversation get totally turned around? They were supposed to be talking about her—not him. "It's a long story. But I really enjoyed the time I spent working with my grandfather. I'll never forget my time at Ristorante Massimo."

"You make it sound like you're leaving."

Dante's fingers tightened on the steering wheel. He had to be more careful with what he said. He could feel her puzzled gaze as she waited for him to affirm or deny her suspicions. That he couldn't do. He hadn't even told his family yet that he was planning to sell the place. There was always one excuse or another to put off the announcement.

But now that the negotiations were winding down, he was out of time. He needed to get his grandfather's blessing to include the family's recipes as part of the sale. Dante's gut tightened.

And the other reason he hesitated to bring it up was that he knew his father would use it as one more thing against him. His father always blamed him for Dante's mother's death during childbirth. Though logically Dante knew he wasn't responsible, he still felt the guilt of playing a part in his father's unhappiness. The man he'd known as a child wore a permanent scowl and he couldn't recall ever seeing his father smile. Not once.

When they communicated it was only because Dante hadn't done a chore or hadn't done it "correctly." Who could blame him for moving away to the city?

But over the years, his father seemed to have changed—mellowed. He wasn't so critical of Dante. But was it enough to rebuild their relationship?

"Dante, are you planning to leave the restaurant? Is that why you're hesitant to help me?"

What was it about this woman that she could read him so well? Too well. "Why would you say that?"

Before she could respond, the strums of music filled the car. He hadn't turned on the stereo and that certainly wasn't his phone's ringtone.

"Oh, no!" Lizzie went diving for her oversize black purse that was on the floor beneath the dash.

"Something wrong?"

"I told my sister to only call me if there was an emergency." She scrambled through her purse. With the phone pressed to her ear, she sounded breathless when she spoke. "Jules, what's the matter?"

Dante glanced at Lizzie, noticing how the color had drained from her face. He wasn't the sort to eavesdrop, but it wasn't as if he could go anywhere. Besides, if she was anything like his younger cousins, it was most likely nothing more than a romantic crisis or a hair emergency—at least he hoped so for Lizzie's sake.

Most of the time when he was out in public, he grew frustrated with people who had their phones turned up so loud that you could hear both sides of the conversation. Lizzie obviously felt the same way as him, as hers was turned down so low that he couldn't hear the caller's voice. Lizzie wasn't much help as she only uttered things like: "Okay."

"Yes."

"Mmm...hmm..."

When her hand started waving around as she talked, Dante didn't know if he should pull over or keep driving.

"He can't do that!"

Who couldn't do what? Was it a boyfriend? Had he done something to her sister? The fact that Lizzie might have a man waiting for her in New York gave him an uneasy sensation.

At last, Lizzie disconnected the call and sank back against the leather upholstery. He wasn't sure what to say because he didn't have a clue what the problem might be. That, and he wasn't very good with upset women. He didn't have much experience in that department as he preferred to keep things light and casual.

Unable to stand the suspense, he asked, "Problems with your boyfriend?"

"Not a chance. I don't have one."

He breathed a little easier. "But I take it there's an emergency?"

"That depends on if you call getting tossed out of your apartment a problem."

"That serious, huh?"

"That man is so greedy, he'd sell his own mother if it'd make him an easy dollar."

"Who's greedy?"

"The landlord. He says he's converting the building into condos."

Dante was truly sorry for Lizzie's plight. He couldn't imagine what it'd be like to get kicked out of your home. Even though he and his father had a tenuous relationship, leaving the vineyard had been completely Dante's idea.

He pulled the car off the road. "Do I need to turn the car around?"

She glanced at him, her brows scrunched up in puzzlement. "Why would you do that?"

"So that you can catch a flight back to New York."

"That's not necessary."

Not necessary. If he was getting evicted, he'd be hightailing it home to find a new place to live. He must be missing something. But what?

"Don't you want to go back and figure out where you're going to live? I can't imagine in such a populated city that it'll be easy to find another place to your liking."

She clucked her tongue. "Are you trying to get rid of me?"

"What?" His tone filled with indignation, but a sliver of guilt sliced through him. "I'm just concerned."

"Well, you don't have to be concerned because the landlord gave us plenty of notice."

"He did?" Lizzie's gaze narrowed on him as he stammered to correct himself. "I...I mean, that's great. Are you sure you'll have time to find another place?"

"My, aren't you worried about my welfare. What

could have brought on this bit of concern? Wait, could it be that you thought this might be your out with the contract?"

"No." The word came out far too fast. He wished he were anywhere but in this much-too-small car. There was nowhere to go. No way to avoid her expectant look. "Okay, it might have crossed my mind. But I still wouldn't wish someone to get kicked out of their home just to save me grief."

She laughed.

The sound grated on his nerves. "What's so funny?"

"The guilty look on your face. You're cute. Like a little boy caught with his hand in the proverbial cookie jar."

Great. Now he'd just been reduced to the level of a cute little kid. Talk about taking direct aim at a guy's ego. He eased the car back onto the road. If he'd ever entertained striking up a more personal relationship with Lizzie, it just came to a screeching halt right there. How did one make a comeback from being "cute"?

"So you aren't mad at me now?" He chanced a quick glance her way as she shook her head.

"I can't blame you for wanting an easy solution to our problem. And after watching how much you worry about your grandfather, I realized that you aren't the sort to revel in others' misfortune."

Wow, she'd read all of that into him not wanting her to drag his grandfather into the middle of their situation? He was truly impressed. But that still didn't erase the *cute little boy* comment. His pride still stung.

After a few moments of silence passed, he turned to the right onto a private lane. "We're here. Are you up for this?"

CHAPTER SEVEN

SHE WAS MOST definitely ready for this adventure.

Lizzie gazed out the car window at the rolling green hills and lines of grapevines. This place was a beauty to behold. Did a more picturesque place exist? She didn't think so.

Of course, it didn't hurt that she was in the most amazing sports car, being escorted by the sexiest man on the planet. But she refused to let Dante know how truly captivated she was by him. She couldn't let him have any more leverage. They still had a contract to iron out.

And whereas he appeared to have plenty of money to hire his own legal dream team, she didn't have two pennies to rub together. She had to play her cards carefully, and by letting him know that she was vulnerable to his gorgeous smile and drawn in by his mesmerizing gaze, she would have lost before she even started.

They pulled to a stop in front of a spacious villa situated atop a hill overlooking the sprawling vineyard and olive grove. The home's lemon-yellow exterior was offset by a red tile roof and pale blue shutters lining the windows and doors. The three-story structure gave off a cheerful appeal that called to Lizzie.

Her gaze came to rest on a sweeping veranda with blue-and-white lawn furniture, which added an inviting quality. What a perfect place to kick back while enjoying a gentle breeze over her sun-warmed skin and sipping an icy lemonade.

"This is where you live?"

Dante cut the engine. "This is where my family lives."

"It's so big."

"It has to be to accommodate so many generations. It seems like every generation expands or adds something."

She especially liked the private balconies. She could easily imagine having her morning coffee there while Dante read the newspaper. "I couldn't even imagine what it would be like to call this my home."

"A little smothering."

"Smothering? You can't be serious." She turned, taking in the endless fields.

He shrugged. "When you have so many people keeping an eye on you constantly, it can be."

"But there's just your grandfather, father and brother, isn't it?"

"You're forgetting about all of my aunts, uncles and cousins. They stop over daily. There's never a lack of relatives. In fact, the dinner table seats twelve and never has an empty chair. They disapproved of my father not remarrying. So they made a point of ensuring my brother and I had a woman's influence."

"And did it work?"

"What? Oh, you mean the woman's-influence thing. I guess it helped. I just know that it was annoying always tripping over family members."

She frowned at him. "You should be grateful that they cared enough!"

His eyes grew round at her agitated tone. "I...I am."

She didn't believe him.

She couldn't even imagine how wonderful it would be to have so much family. He took it all for granted, not having sense enough to count his blessings. She'd have done anything to have a big, loving family.

"Not everyone is as lucky as you." With that,

she got out of the car, no longer wanting to hear how hard Dante had it putting up with his relatives.

He was the luckiest person she knew. He wasn't much older than herself and he already owned his very own restaurant—a successful one at that. Not to mention his jaw-dropping apartment. And she couldn't forget his flashy sports car. And on top of all that, he had a family that cared about him. Stacked up against her life, she was left lacking. She was up to her eyeballs in debt. And without the money from this television spot, she didn't know how she'd survive.

But how did she explain any of that to him? How would he ever understand when he couldn't even appreciate what he had? She'd met people like him before—specifically a guy in college. He was an only child—and spoiled. He thought he understood what hardship was when he had to buy a used car to replace the brand-new one his parents had bought him—a car he'd wrecked while out partying with the guys. She stifled the groan of frustration that rose in her throat. Hardship was choosing between paying the rent or buying groceries.

A gentle breeze brushed over her cheeks and

whipped her hair into her face. She tucked the loose strands behind her ear. The air felt good. It eased her tense muscles, sweeping up her frustration and carrying it away.

In this particular case, she'd overreacted. Big-time. She had better keep a firmer grip on her emotions or soon Dante would learn about her past. She didn't want him to look down on her like she was less than everyone else since her mother hadn't loved her enough to straighten out her life and her father was someone without a name—a face. The breath caught in her throat.

She hated that being around Dante was bringing all of these old feelings of inadequacy to the surface. She'd buried them long ago. Coming here was a mistake. Nursing her dream of finding out what it would be like to have a grandfather—a family—was opening Pandora's box and her past was spilling out.

What had set her off?

Dante darted out of the car, but then froze. Lizzie's back was to him. Her shoulders were rigid. Her head was held high. He didn't want to do battle with her. Especially not here, where his family could happen upon them at any moment.

But more than that, he didn't have a clue what he'd done wrong. Did she have that strong an opinion about families? And if so, why?

His questions about her only multiplied. And as much as he'd set out to learn more about his flat-mate on the ride here, he truly believed he had gained more questions than answers. Sure, he'd learned that she appeared to be very close with her sister and that she was about to get evicted. Oh, and she was a stickler for following the rules—especially the rules of the road. But there was so much more she was holding back. Things he wanted to know. But that would have to wait.

He could only hope that he could smooth things over with her before his father descended upon them. He didn't need her giving his family the impression that he didn't know how to treat a lady. His father already held enough things against him without adding to the list.

He rounded the car and stopped in front of her. "Hey, I don't know what I said back there, but I'm sorry. You must miss your family."

Her head lowered and her shoulders drooped. "It's me that should apologize. I guess it was just hearing Jules's voice made me realize it's going to be a long time before I will see her again. We've never been apart for an extended period like this."

So that was it. She was homesick. That was totally understandable. Maybe his family could help fill that gap. They certainly were a chatty, friendly bunch—even if they could be a bit over-bearing at times.

"Why don't we go inside? I'm sure my father and brother are out in the fields. They keep a close eye on the vines and soil. But my grandfather will be around. Not to mention an aunt or two."

She smiled. "Thanks for including me. I'm really excited to meet your family."

"They're looking forward to meeting you, too."

"They know I'm coming?" When he nodded, she said, "But you made it sound like you'd planned to come without me."

"I had, but my grandfather had other ideas. He insisted I bring you to meet him. He told the family while I was on the phone."

"Would you have really left me behind if I hadn't promised to keep quiet about the contract?"

Dante shrugged. "I guess we'll never know. Just remember our agreement. Don't say or do anything to upset my grandfather."

Her eyes flared with indignation. But before she could say a word, there were footsteps on the gravel.

"Dante, who's your guest?"

He didn't even have to turn around to recognize his older brother's voice. Stefano was the eldest. The son who did no wrong. He'd stayed on at the villa and helped their father run the vineyard as was expected of the DeFiore men. But what no one took into consideration was that Stefano always got along with their father. He wasn't the one their father held responsible for their mother's death.

Dante turned on his heels. "Stefano, this is Lizzie."

Stefano stepped up, and when she extended her hand, he accepted it and kissed the back of it. Dante's blood pressure spiked. What was his brother doing? Wasn't he the forlorn widower?

Not that Dante wished for his brother to be miserable the rest of his life. In fact, he wished that Stefano would be able to move past the nightmare and get on with his life, but Stefano seemed certain that he would remain a bachelor...which seemed to be the destiny of the DeFiore men.

Dante had learned much from his family, especially to keep his guard up around women. He had zero intention of getting caught up in the tangled web of love. It only led to pain. Something he could live without.

While Stefano made idle chitchat with Lizzie, Dante noticed how her face lit up. He swallowed down his agitation. "Is Nonno in the house?"

Stefano turned to him. His whole demeanor changed into something more stoic—more like the brother he knew. "Of course. Where else would you expect him to be?"

Dante rolled his eyes and started for the house. When he realized that Lizzie had remained behind with his brother, he turned and signaled for her to follow him. She smiled at Stefano—a great big, ear-to-ear, genuine smile that lit up the world like a starburst. Dante's jaw tightened.

Why couldn't she be that happy around him? Why did she have to act so reserved—so on guard? After all, he was a nice guy, too. Or so he'd been told by some lady friends. Surely he hadn't lost his touch with the women. Maybe he'd have to try a little harder.

When Lizzie joined him, he said, "My grandfather is probably getting impatient. We should go see him."

Lizzie kept her smile in place and he couldn't help but wonder if it was part of their agreement to keep the mood light and happy. Or perhaps it was lingering happiness from meeting his older brother—Mr. Tall, Dark and Persuasive.

Not that it mattered if Lizzie had a thing for Stefano. It wasn't as if Dante was interested in the woman who was threatening the deal he'd been working for weeks to finalize. And it rankled him that he now felt some sort of responsibility toward Lizzie. Not only did he have to take into consideration what was best for the business, but also he felt compelled to take into account how it impacted her.

Dante stepped into the sunroom. "Nonno."

His grandfather's silver head lifted from reading a newspaper. He removed his reading glasses, focused on Dante and then his gaze moved to Lizzie. A lopsided smile pulled at his lips. Dante inwardly sighed at the effect Lizzie had over the men in his family. They stared at her as if she were a movie star. Well…she was pretty enough. Still, they didn't have to act as though they'd never seen a beautiful female before. Then again, it had been a very long time since a woman that wasn't a relative had visited the DeFiore villa. Okay, so maybe they had a reason to sit up and take notice. He just wished they didn't make it so noticeable.

"Come here." Nonno's deep voice was a bit slurred from the stroke.

His grandfather's gaze clung to Lizzie. She moved forward without hesitation and came to a stop in front of his chair. Then something happened that totally surprised Dante. She bent over and hugged his grandfather. It was as though they'd known each other forever. How did that happen?

The two of them chatted while Dante sat on the couch. He really wasn't needed as neither of them even noticed that he was in the room. And he could plainly see that Lizzie's presence had an uplifting effect on his grandfather. In fact, this was the happiest he'd seen his grandfather since he'd been forced into retirement.

"So that's why you changed your mind about visiting this weekend?" Dante's father entered the room and came to a stop by the couch before nodding in Lizzie's direction.

Dante instinctively followed his father's gaze back to the woman who'd thrown his life into turmoil. "She knows Nonno. He asked me to bring her here."

His father nodded. "If I had that sort of distraction, I might stay in the city, too. After all, it's a lot easier to have a good time with a beautiful woman than it is to do the hard work needed to keep the family vineyard running."

Dante's jaw ratcheted tight. It didn't matter what he said; it never seemed to be the right thing where his father was concerned. Some things never changed.

"At least you have good taste." That was the closest his father had ever come to giving him a compliment.

"Lizzie and I are working together, nothing more."

His father sent him a *you are crazy* look. Dante wasn't going to argue with the man—it wouldn't change things. He never lived up to his father's expectations—not like his brother, Stefano, always did. Just once, he'd like his father to clap him on the back and tell him he'd done something right—something good.

Dante sat rigidly on the couch. Not even his father's jabs were enough to make him leave the room. He assured himself that it was just to keep an eye on what Lizzie said to his grandfather. Because there couldn't be any other reason.

Unlike the rest of his family, he was immune to her charms.

Sure, he knew how to enjoy a woman's company. Her smiles. Her laugh. Her touch. But that was as far as it went. He refused to let himself become vulnerable. He'd seen too much pain in his life. It wouldn't happen to him. The *L* word wasn't worth the staggering risks.

CHAPTER EIGHT

"THIS PLACE IS AMAZING."

Lizzie didn't bother to hide her enthusiasm as she glanced around the spacious living room with a high ceiling and two sets of double doors that let the afternoon sun stream in. She'd trade her Bronx apartment in a heartbeat for this peaceful retreat.

"I love it here." She spoke the words to no one in particular. "Very different from city life."

"It is different." Massimo's words took her full attention between the accent and the slight slur from his stroke. "I'm glad you're here. Is my grandson treating you well?"

Her thoughts flashed back to their first meeting. But she wasn't so sure that Massimo would find it amusing that Dante mistook her presence at the restaurant and put her to work as a hostess. She opted to save that story for a later date.

She glanced across to where Dante was pretending to read a cooking magazine. "Yes. He...he's been a gentleman."

Massimo gave her a quizzical look. "My grandson is a good man. He knows a lot. Make him teach you."

His choice of words struck her as a bit odd. Either the man was eager to shorten his sentences or he sensed that things between her and Dante weren't going smoothly.

"I will. I just wish you could be there. I was really looking forward to working next to such a legend."

Massimo attempted to smile but the one side of his mouth would not cooperate. Her heart pinched. She had no idea how frustrating it must be for your body not to cooperate. But beyond that, the man's face spoke of exhaustion. Dante had warned her not to overtax him. And she wouldn't do anything to harm Massimo. The place in her heart for him had only grown exponentially since meeting him in person.

"I'll let you get some rest." Lizzie went to stand when Massimo reached for her hand.

His grip was strong but not painful. But it was the look in his eyes that dug at her heart. "Promise me you won't give up. Promise me you'll see through our deal."

"But—" She'd almost uttered the fact that Dante

was opposed to the whole idea. "I'll do my best." It was all she could offer the man.

"My grandson needs someone like you."

The following morning Lizzie hit the ground running.

She wasn't about to waste a minute of her time at the villa. The big, brilliant ball of orange was still low in the distant horizon. She stood just outside the kitchen door with a cup of steamy black coffee in hand.

She wandered across to an old wooden fence and gazed out at the endless acres of grapes. The golden rays gave the rows and rows of vines a beauty all of their own. She'd never been someplace so wide open. She reveled in the peacefulness that surrounded her. And that was something she truly found amazing. Normally her nights were full of restless dreams and her days full of running here and there, doing this and that. But here she could take a moment to breathe—just to be.

Her thoughts trailed back to her unusual conversation with Massimo. Was the man some sort of matchmaker? But why? He hardly knew her. How would he know if she would be good for Dante? And why would Dante need her?

The questions followed one after the other. The most frustrating part was that she didn't have an answer for any of them. Dante was even more of a mystery to her now than he was before.

She'd noticed from the moment they'd arrived here that everything wasn't so perfect in Dante's life. Though she hadn't been able to hear the conversation between father and son, she'd clearly seen the dark look that had come over Dante's handsome face while talking with his father. There was a definite distance between him and his family. Was that what Massimo thought she could help Dante with? But how? She was here for only a matter of weeks, certainly not long enough to change someone's life. And what did she know about the inner workings of families?

Still, she couldn't get her mind to stop replaying the events from the prior evening. When his family grew boisterous talking of the vineyard, she noticed how Dante had become withdrawn as if he didn't feel as though he fit in—or was it that he didn't want to fit in? Either way, she couldn't imagine Dante willingly walking away from such an amazing place.

There had to be something more to his story—something he wasn't willing to share. But what could drive him from the peacefulness of the countryside and the bosom of his family to the city? Unless… Was it possible? Her mind raced. Could he have a passion for cooking that rivaled hers? Was it possible that they at last had something in common?

The thunk of the kitchen door swinging shut startled her. She spun around and there stood the man who'd filled her every thought since arriving here. The heat crept up her neck and settled in her cheeks. She realized that she was being silly. It wasn't as if he could read her mind.

Their gazes met and held. His stare was deep and probing. Unease inched up her spine. There was no way that he could know that just moments ago, she'd been daydreaming about his grandfather's suggestion that she and Dante might be a perfect fit.

"I didn't know if you'd be up yet." His voice was deep and gravelly.

"I set my phone alarm. I didn't want to miss the sunrise."

"And was it worth the effort?"

She nodded vigorously. "Definitely. I'm in love."

When his eyes widened in surprise, she added, "With the villa and the vineyard. With all of it."

"I'm glad you like it here."

"I was considering going for a walk."

"Would you care for some company?"

Her gaze jerked back around to his to see if he was serious. "You really want to escort me around? I mean, it isn't like I'll be running into any of your family. You don't have to babysit me."

"I didn't offer so I could play babysitter. I thought maybe you'd want some company, but obviously I was wrong." He turned back to the house.

"Wait." He paused, but he didn't turn around. She swallowed down a chunk of pride. "I would like your company."

He turned to her but his lips were pressed together in a firm line. He crossed his arms and looked at her expectantly. He had a right to expect more. She'd been snippy and he hadn't deserved it. But it wasn't easy for her. For some reason, she had the hardest time dealing with him. His mere presence put her on edge. And he always scattered her thoughts with his good looks and charming smile.

"Okay, I'm sorry. Is that what you want to hear?"

"Yes, it is." He stepped up to her. "Shall we go?"

She glanced down at the almost empty cup. "I need to put this in the house."

He took it from her, jogged back to the kitchen and returned in no time. He extended his arm like a total gentleman, which sent her heart tumbling in her chest. Without hesitation, she slipped her hand into the crook of his arm. When her fingers tightened around his biceps, she noticed his rock-hard strength.

This wasn't right. She had no business letting her guard down around him. Nothing good would come of it. She considered pulling away, but part of her refused to let go. With a quick glance at his relaxed features, she realized she was making too much of the situation.

He led her away from the house and down a dirt path. "You made quite an impression on my family."

"Is that a good thing?"

"Most definitely. They're all quite taken with you. It was the most excitement they've had around here in quite a while."

Normally she kept up her walls and held everyone at bay, but being here, being around Massimo, she'd let down her defenses a bit. "I noticed you were quiet last night. Was there something wrong?"

"No, not at all. And you were amazing, especially with Nonno. He's been really down in the dumps, but you cheered him up. So I owe you a big thank-you."

She noticed how he didn't explain his quietness. She wondered if he was always so reserved around his family. Granted, she didn't understand how traditional families worked as her life had consisted of foster homes where kids came and went and there wasn't that deep, abiding love that came naturally. But she had Jules and they were as close as any blood relatives.

"Your brother, he's older than you, isn't he?" She wanted to get Dante to open up about his family. She couldn't help it. She was curious.

"Yes. He's a couple of years older."

Well, that certainly didn't strike up the hoped-for conversation. "Are you two very close?"

Dante slanted a gaze her way but she pretended not to notice. "I don't know. We're brothers."

She knew none of this was any of her business but everything about Dante intrigued her. He was like an artichoke and she'd barely begun to pull at the tough outer layer. There was so much to learn before she got to the tender center that he protected from everyone.

"They care a lot about you."

He stopped and pulled her around to look at him. "Why all of this curiosity about my family? What's going on in that beautiful mind of yours?"

Did he just say she was beautiful? Her gaze met his and her breath became shallow. No, he'd said her mind was beautiful. But was that the same thing as saying she was beautiful?

"I was just making small talk." She tried to act innocent. "Why do I have to have ulterior motives?"

"I didn't say you did. But sometimes you make me wonder." He peered into her eyes and for a moment she wondered if he could read her thoughts.

Heat filled her cheeks and she glanced away. "Wonder about what?"

"You. There's more to you than meets the eye. Something tells me that you have an interesting past."

She couldn't hold back a laugh. "You make me sound very mysterious. Like Mata Hari or something." She leaned closer to him and whispered in his ear. "I'm here to find out your secrets."

He grabbed her upper arms and moved her back,

allowing her the opportunity to see the worry lines ingrained on his face. "What secrets?"

His hard, sharp tone startled her. "Your secrets in the kitchen, of course. What else did you think I meant?"

His frown eased. "You're having far too much fun at my expense."

So the man was keeping secrets. From her? Or from the whole world? She didn't think it was possible but she was even more intrigued by him.

She gazed into his bottomless brown eyes. "You need to let your hair down and have some fun. It won't hurt. I promise."

"Is that what all of the smiling and laughing was about last night? Or are you trying to sway my family over to your side so they'll pressure me into agreeing to follow through with the contract?"

She pulled back her shoulders. She knew she shouldn't but she just couldn't help herself. His gaze dipped as her fingers once again made an X over her chest. "I promised not to do that."

The vein in his neck pulsated and when his eyes met hers again, there was a need, a passion in his gaze. Her line of vision dipped to his lips.

"You do know that you're driving me crazy, don't you?"

"Who, me?" This was the most fun she'd ever had. She'd never flirted with a guy before. Sure, they'd flirted with her but she never felt the desire to return the flirtations.

Until now.

His hands encircled her waist. "Yes, you. Do you have any idea what I'd like to do to you right now?"

A few scintillating thoughts danced and teased her mind. She placed her hands on his chest and felt the pounding of his heart. She was certain that hers could easily keep time with his. It was pumping so fast that it felt as if she'd just finished a long run on a hot, muggy day. In that moment she was overcome by the urge to find out if his kiss was as moving in real life as it had been in her dreams last night.

"You know, we really shouldn't do this." His voice was carried like a whisper in the breeze.

"When have you ever done what was expected of you?"

"Not very often." His gaze bored deep into her, making her stomach quiver with need.

"Then why start now? I won't tell, if you won't."

That was all it took. His head dipped and then his lips were there. He stopped just a breath away from hers. She could practically feel the turbulent vibes coming off him. It was as though he was fighting an inner battle between what was right and what he wanted. She needed to put him out of his misery—out of her misery.

Acting on total instinct and desire, she leaned up on her tiptoes and pressed her mouth to his. His lips were smooth and warm. He didn't move. He wanted it. She knew that as well as she knew that the sun would set that evening. Perhaps he needed just a touch more enticement.

She let her body lean into his as her hands slipped up over his broad shoulders. Her fingertips raked through his dark hair as her lips gently moved over his. And then she heard a hungry moan swell in his throat as he pulled her snug against him.

Perhaps it was the knowledge that this kiss should be forbidden that made it the most enticing kiss she'd ever experienced. Then again, it could be that she was lonely and missing her sister, and being in Dante's arms made her feel connected to someone. Or maybe it was simply the fact that he was the dreamiest hunk she'd ever laid her eyes on, and she just wanted to see what she'd be missing by holding herself back.

He stroked and prodded, sending her heart pounding against her ribs with pure desire. His hard planes fit perfectly against her soft curves. And for the moment, she felt like the most beautiful—most desired—woman in the world.

Dante moved, placing his hands on each side of her face. When he pulled his lips from hers, she felt bereft. She wanted more. Needed more.

He rested his forehead against hers. His breathing was deep and uneven. He'd been just as caught up in the moment as she'd been, so why had he stopped? What had happened?

His thumb gently stroked her cheek. "Lizzie, we can't do this. You know that it's wrong."

"But it felt so right."

She couldn't help it. She wasn't ready for the harsh light of reality. She lived every single day with the sharp edges of reality slicing into her dreams. Just once, she wanted to know what it was like not to have to worry about meeting the monthly bills. She just wanted this one blissful memory.

"Lizzie, this can't happen. You and I…it's impossible."

His words pricked her bubble of happiness. Once again she was being rejected. And the worst part was he was right. And that thought made the backs of her eyes sting.

When was it going to be her turn for just a little bit of happiness without the rug being pulled out from under her? This trip to Rome should be the trip of a lifetime, but now the entire arrangement was in jeopardy and she had no job to return to.

She blinked repeatedly, keeping the moisture in her eyes in check. If she was good at one thing in life, it was being a trooper. When life dropped lemons on her, she whipped up a lemon meringue pie with the fluffiest, tallest peaks. She could do it again.

She pulled back until her spine was straight and his hands fell away. "You're right. I don't know what I was thinking." Her voice wobbled. She swallowed down the lump of emotion. "It won't happen again."

Without meeting his gaze, she moved past him and started for the villa. The tip of her tongue ran over her lower lip, where she found the slightest minty taste of toothpaste he'd left behind. She stifled a frustrated moan, knowing that he was only a few steps behind her.

CHAPTER NINE

HE'D TOTALLY BLOWN IT.

Dante stowed their bags in the car's boot and then glanced back at the villa. Lizzie smiled at his grandfather before hugging him goodbye. A stab of jealousy tore into Dante. She'd barely spoken to him after they'd kissed, and even then, it'd only been one-word answers. Why in the world had he let his hormones do the thinking for him?

He had absolutely no desire to toy with her feelings. Hurting Lizzie was the last thing in the world he wanted to do. And though she appeared to have it all together, he knew that she had a vulnerable side, too. He'd witnessed the hurt that had flashed in her eyes when she realized that he didn't trust her with his grandfather. She wanted him to think she was tough, but he knew lurking beneath the beautiful surface lay a vulnerable woman—a woman that he was coming to like a bit more than he should.

When she at last joined him in the car, she

stared straight ahead. The unease between them was palpable. Dante didn't like it one bit, but he had no one to blame but himself. There was no way he could go back in time and undo the kiss. And if he could, he wasn't so sure he would. Their kiss had been something special—something he'd never experienced before.

He cut his thoughts off short. He realized that it was thoughts like this that had gotten him into trouble in the first place. But he couldn't ignore the fact that this silent treatment was doing him in.

"Are you ever going to speak to me again?" He struggled to keep the frustration out of his voice.

"Yes."

More of the one-syllable answers. "Did you enjoy your visit to the vineyard?"

"Yes."

"Enough with the yeses and nos." His hands tightened on the steering wheel, trying to get a grip on his rising frustration. Worst of all was the fact he had no clue how to fix things between them. And whether it was wise or not, he wanted Lizzie to like him. "My grandfather seemed quite taken with you. In fact, the whole family did."

Nothing.

She crossed her arms and huffed. What did that mean? Was she about to let him have it? His muscles tensed as he waited for a tongue-lashing. Not that he could blame her. He deserved it, but it wouldn't make it any less uncomfortable.

Her voice was soft and he strained to hear her. "How do you do it?"

Well, it was more than one syllable, but he didn't have a clue what she meant. And he was hesitant to ask, but what choice did he have?

"How do I do what?" The breath caught in his throat as he waited for what came next.

"How do you drive away from that little piece of heaven at the end of each weekend and return to the city?"

This wasn't the direction he'd expected the conversation to take. His family wasn't a subject he talked about beyond the generalities. *How's your father? Is your brother still working at the vineyard? Did they have a good harvest?* But no one ever probed into his choice to move away—to distance himself from his family.

"I prefer Rome." It wasn't necessarily a lie.

"Don't get me wrong. I love the city life. But I was born and bred in a city that never sleeps. I think it's in my bones to appreciate the chatter of voices and the hum of vehicles. But you, you were raised in the peace and tranquillity."

"It isn't the perfect slice of heaven like you're thinking." He tried not to think about his childhood. He didn't want to remember.

"What wasn't perfect about it?"

He glanced her way, giving her a warning stare to leave the subject alone.

"Hey, you're the one who wanted me to talk. I'm talking. Now it's your turn."

He could see that she wasn't going to leave this subject alone. Not unless he let her know that she was stepping on a very tender subject.

"Life at the DeFiore Vineyard wasn't idyllic when I was a kid. Far from it."

"Why?"

She really was going to push this. And for some unknown reason, he wanted to make her understand his side. "I'm the reason my mother died."

"What?" She swung around in her seat, fighting with the seat belt so that she was able to look directly at him. "But I don't understand. How?"

"She died after she gave birth to me."

"Oh. How horrible." There was an awkward pause. "But it wasn't your fault."

"No, not directly. But my father blamed me. He told me that I took away the best part of his life."

"He didn't mean it. That…those words, they were part of his grief."

Dante shoved his fingers through his hair. "He meant it. I can't help but feel that I bring sadness and misery to those closest to me—"

"Nonsense. Listen, I'm so sorry for your loss. I know how tough that can be, but you're not to blame for her death or how your father handled his grief. We all handle the death of family members differently."

That caught his attention. A chance to turn the tables away from himself and back to her. "Have you lost a parent?"

Silence enveloped the car. Only the hum of the engine and the tires rolling over the blacktop could be heard. Lizzie turned away to stare out the side window as Dante drove on, waiting and wondering.

"Lizzie, you can talk to me. Whatever you say won't go any further."

He took his focus off the road for just a moment to glance her way. She cast him a hesitant look. He had a feeling she had something important to say—something she didn't normally share. He really hoped she'd let down her guard and let him in. He wanted so badly to understand more about her.

"My mother died." Her voice was so soft.

"I'm sorry. I guess we've both had some hard knocks in life."

"Yes, but at least you have a loving family. And you can always go home when you want to..." It seemed as though she wanted to say more but stopped.

This conversation was much deeper—much more serious than he'd ever expected. He wanted to press for more information, but he sensed now wasn't the time. Spotting a small village up ahead with a trattoria, he slowed down.

"You know, we left without eating. Would you care for a bite of food? And they have the best *caffé* around. I noticed that you have quite a fondness for cappuccino."

"I do. And I'd love to get some."

He eased off the road and maneuvered the car into the lot. Before he got out, he knew there was something more he had to say. "I'm sorry about what happened back at the vineyard. The kiss was a mistake. I didn't mean to cross the line. The last thing I want to do is hurt you."

She turned to him and smiled, but the gesture never quite reached her eyes. "Don't worry. You'd have to do a lot more than that kiss to hurt me. Now let's get that coffee."

Without giving him a chance to say anything else, she alighted from the car. Her words might have been what he wanted to hear, but he didn't believe her. His gut told him that he'd hurt her more deeply than her stubborn pride would let on.

He didn't know what it was about Ms. Lizzie Addler from New York, but she was getting to him. He longed to be a good guy in her eyes, but he was torn between his desire to help her and his need to sell the *ristorante* in order to return to the vineyard and help his family. How was he supposed to make everyone happy? Was it even possible?

How had that happened?

Lizzie had entered the quaint restaurant with no appetite at all. And now as they exited the small family establishment, her stomach was full up with the most delicious sampling of pastas, meats and cheeses.

It had all started when they'd been greeted by the sweetest older woman. She'd insisted that they have a seat while she called to her husband, who was in the kitchen. Apparently they'd known Dante all of his life and were thrilled to see that he'd brought his lady friend to meet them. When Lizzie tried to correct the very chatty woman, her words got lost in the conversation.

"Are they always so outgoing?" Lizzie asked Dante as they approached the car.

"Guido and Luiso Caruso have known my family for years, and yes, they are always that friendly. Did you get enough to eat?"

Lizzie gently patted her rounded stomach. "I'm stuffed."

Dante snapped his fingers. "I forgot to give them a message from my grandfather. I'll be right back."

While Dante rushed back inside, Lizzie leaned against the car's fender and lifted her face to the sun. Perhaps she was hungrier than she thought because now that she'd eaten, her mood was much lighter. And it'd helped that Dante had opened up to her about his family. No matter how little he cracked open the door to his past, every bit he shared meant a lot to her.

But nothing could dislodge the memory of that earth-shattering kiss. It was always there, lurking around the edges of her mind. But the part that stung was how Dante had rejected her. And his reasoning did nothing to soothe her.

Somehow she'd get past this crazy infatuation. Because in the end, he was right. They did have to work together over the next eight weeks. Not to mention that they shared an apartment—anything else, no matter how casual, would just complicate matters.

"Ready to go?" Dante frowned as he noticed her leaning against the flawless paint job.

"Yes, I am."

As he got closer, she noticed how he inspected where she'd been leaning, as if she'd dented the car or something. His hand smoothed across the paint.

"Are you serious?" she asked incredulously.

He turned to her, his face perfectly serious. "What?"

He really didn't get it. She smiled and shook her head. Men and their cars. "Nothing."

"If we get going we should be home in no time. There's not much traffic. And the weather is perfect." He repeatedly tossed the keys in the air.

Lizzie moved in to catch them. "Let me drive."

"What? You're joking, right?" He reached out to take the keys from her.

She pulled her hand behind her back, which drew her blouse tight across her chest. His gaze dipped and lingered just a moment. When his gaze met hers again, she smiled.

"Come on. You said yourself there is hardly any traffic."

And she'd love to drive an honest-to-goodness exclusive sports car, the kind that turned heads—both men and women, young and old. She may not be a car junkie, but that didn't mean she couldn't appreciate a fine vehicle. And this car was quite fine. Jules would never believe she'd gotten to drive such an amazing sports car.

"I don't think so." The smile slipped from his face. "Can I have the keys so we can get going?"

Enjoying having him at a disadvantage, she felt her smile broaden. She backed up a few steps. She was in the mood to have a little fun, hoping it'd get them back on track. "If you want them, you'll have to come and get them."

He didn't move. "This isn't funny." His tone grew quite insistent. "Hand over the keys."

Her good mood screeched to a halt. He wouldn't even consider letting her behind the steering wheel. Did he really think so little of her that she couldn't drive a car in a straight line?

Hurt balled up in her gut. She dropped the keys in his outstretched hand and strode around the car. "I assume I'm still allowed to sit in the passenger seat."

"Hey, you don't have to be like that. After all, I don't let anyone drive Red."

Her head snapped around to face him. "You named your car?"

"Of course. Why wouldn't I?"

She shook her head, having no words to describe her amazement.

"Besides, I'm sure that you'll enjoy riding in the passenger seat more. You can take a nap or check out the passing scenery."

It hurt her how easily he brushed off her request as though she couldn't possibly be serious about wanting to drive such a fine machine. All of her life people had never seen past her foster-kid status and used clothes. Even now as she sat on the butter-soft upholstery of a car that she would never be able to afford in her entire life, she was wearing hand-me-downs. But at least these clothes fit her and they didn't look as though they'd seen a better day.

She was tired of people underestimating her. She refused to sit by and take it. She would show Dante that she was just as capable as him.

CHAPTER TEN

"I KEPT MY WORD."

The sound of Lizzie's voice startled Dante.

She'd resumed her quiet mode after he'd asked for the keys. He had no idea she was so intent on driving his car—his gem. She obviously didn't know how precious it was to him and he didn't know how to describe it to her. The fact that his father liked this car almost as much as Dante did meant the world to him. And the fact that he'd bought it all on his own had earned him some of his father's respect. He couldn't afford to lose that one small step.

Dante unlocked the penthouse door. "You kept your word about what?"

"The contract. I didn't say a word while we were at the villa. But now that we're back and the film crew will be here tomorrow at 6:00 a.m., I need to know if you're on board with the whole thing." Lizzie strode into the living room. She fished around in her purse, eventually producing her cell phone. Her gaze met his as her finger hovered over the touch screen.

His curiosity was piqued. "Who are you planning to call?"

"My contact at the studio."

"Did you already tell them about my grandfather not being able to fulfill his obligation?"

She nodded. "I told them right away."

He kind of figured she would. "And what did they say?"

He wasn't so sure he wanted to hear the answer because Lizzie looked far too confident. What did she know that he didn't?

Lizzie perched on the arm of the couch. "They were sorry to hear about your grandfather."

"And?"

"And when I mentioned that you'd taken over the restaurant, they were intrigued. They pulled up some old footage of you with your grandfather and they're convinced transitioning the spotlight from your grandfather to you will work."

He should have known that eventually being on television even for a few seconds would come back to bite him. He just never expected this. Who would want him on television? He knew nothing of acting. And he wasn't inclined to learn.

"Lizzie, I haven't agreed to this. Any of it." And he didn't want to either.

"But what choice do you have at this point? If your attorney was going to uncover an easy out, he'd have told you by now."

Dante's hands pressed down on the granite countertop. He wanted to argue with her. He wanted to point out that this idea didn't have a chance to be a success. But even his solicitor wasn't rushing in, promising that all would be fine. In fact, his solicitor had said quite the opposite. That trying to break the contract would cost him money and time.

The television exposure would definitely give the *ristorante* added publicity and the asking price could easily be inflated. As it was, he'd been forced to lower the price to unload it quickly, but now there wouldn't be a rush. He could ask for a more realistic price and perhaps someone else would step forward that would want the *ristorante* without buying the family recipes.

Lizzie tossed her oversize purse on the couch. "Besides, if you help me out, I'll help you out."

"What do you have in mind?"

"If you agree to do the filming each morning

before the restaurant opens, I can help you around Ristorante Massimo."

His brows rose. "You're offering to work for me?"

"Sure. What else do I have to do with my time?"

There had to be a catch. There always was. Everybody wanted something. "And what are you expecting me to pay you?"

She shrugged. "Nothing."

"Nothing?"

"I'd just like a chance to do what I would have done with your grandfather."

"And that was?"

"To learn from him. He was planning to teach me as much as he could while I was in town. I came to Italy with the sole intent to work my butt off."

Dante eyed her up. "You really don't want anything else but to learn?"

"Why do you sound so skeptical?"

He shrugged. "I'm not used to people offering me free help."

"I wouldn't get used to it. Not everyone can afford to do it. But the studio is paying me to be here, and with you providing free room and board, it should all work out."

At last he found the rub. "You intend to continue to live here? With me?"

"Is this your way of saying that you plan to kick me out?"

"You have to admit that after what happened in the vineyard the idea of us living and working together isn't a good one."

"Why? Are you saying that you want to repeat that kiss?" She moved forward, only stopping when she stood on the other side of the counter. "Are you wishing that you hadn't stopped it?"

His gaze dipped to her pink frosted lips. Oh, yes, he definitely wanted to continue that kiss. He wanted it to go on and on. "No. That's not what I'm saying. Quit putting words in my mouth."

Her eyes flashed her disbelief. "I only call 'em like I see 'em."

"It has nothing to do with the kiss. I'd already forgotten about it." No, he hadn't. Not in the least. "It's just…"

"Just what?" Lines bracketed her icy blue eyes as she waited for his answer.

"I just don't know if you understand what will be expected from you."

"You mean you think I'm just another pretty face without anything between my ears."

"Hey, I didn't say that. There you go again, making assumptions."

"Then what did you mean?"

"I have my way of doing things. And I expect you to pay attention to the details—no matter how small or meaningless you might find them." He needed time alone to get his head on straight. There was a lot here to consider. "I'm going to my office. We'll talk more later."

"Do you mind if I go downstairs and have a look around. I want to know what I'm getting myself into."

"Be my guest. Here's the key." He tossed her a key card and rattled off the security pass code.

Her lips pressed into a firm line as she clutched the key card and turned for the door. He stood there in the kitchenette. He couldn't turn away as his gaze was latched on the gentle sway of her hips as she strode away. His pulse raced and memories of holding her and tasting her sweet kisses clouded his mind. How had he ever found the willpower to let her go?

The snick of the door closing snapped Dante back to the here and now. What was so different about her? He'd dated his share of women and none of them had gotten to him like her. But if there was any possibility of them working together and sharing this apartment, he needed to see her as just another coworker. Someone who couldn't get under his skin and give him that overwhelming urge to scratch his itch. Because that would only lead them both into trouble as had already happened back at the vineyard.

He should just show Lizzie the door and forget trying to fulfill his grandfather's wishes. If he was logical, that was what he'd do. But when it came to family, nothing was logical.

Combine that with the desperation he'd witnessed in Lizzie's gaze, and he felt an overwhelming urge to find a way to make this work for both of them. But could he keep his hormones in check around her? Suddenly his apartment wasn't looking so big after all.

She'd prove him wrong.

Lizzie strode into the impressive kitchen of Ristorante Massimo. It was more spacious than it had appeared on television. And she immediately felt at home surrounded by the stainless-steel appliances. She just wished that Massimo would be there instead of his stubborn grandson.

But she had a plan. She was going to prove to Dante that she was talented—that she could hold up her end of the agreement. She looked over the ingredients in the fridge and the freezer. Slowly a dinner menu took shape in her mind. She didn't want it to be pasta as she didn't want to compete in his arena. No, she would whip up something else.

She set to work, anxious to prove to Dante that she belonged here in Massimo's kitchen. She had the ability; she just needed to broaden her horizons with new culinary skills.

She didn't know how much time had passed when she heard a sound behind her. She turned and jumped when she saw Dante propping himself up in the doorway.

"What are you doing there?" She set aside the masher she'd used to whip up the cauliflower.

"I think I'm the one who should be asking you that question."

She glanced around at the mess she'd created. Okay, so she wasn't the neatest person in the kitchen. But to be honest, she had seen worse. And she was in a hurry. She'd wanted it all to be completed before he arrived. So much for her plan.

"I thought I'd put together dinner."

He walked closer. "And what's on the menu?"

She ran over and pressed a hand to his chest to stop him. The warmth from his body and the rhythm of his heart sent tingles shooting up her arm. Big mistake. But her heart wasn't listening to her head. A bolt of awareness struck her and all she could think about was stepping a little closer. The breath caught in her throat as she looked up at his tempting lips.

Memories of his caresses dominated her thoughts. She'd never been kissed like that before. It had meaning. It had depth. And it had left her longing for more. But this wasn't the time or the place. She had to make a point with him. And caving in to her desires would not help her cause.

She pulled her hand back. "I have a table all set in the dining room. Why don't you go make yourself comfortable? The food will be in shortly."

He strained his neck, looking around. "Are you sure I shouldn't stay and help?"

She pressed her hands to her hips. "I'm positive. Go."

He hesitated and she started to wonder if he was going to trust her. But then he relented. And turned. When he exited the kitchen, she rushed to finish up with the things on the stove. She placed them in the oven to keep them warm.

At last, it was time to start serving up the most important meal of her life. Since when had impressing Dante become more about what he thought of her and less about gaining the job? She consoled herself with the thought that it was just nerves. It wasn't as if he was the first man to kiss her. Nor would he be the last.

She pushed aside the jumbled thoughts as she moved to the refrigerator and removed the crab-and-avocado salad. She placed the dish on the tray, took off her apron and smoothed a hand over her hair, worrying that she must look a mess. Oh, well, it was too late to worry about it now.

Then, realizing that she'd forgotten something for him to drink, she grabbed both a glass of chilled water and a bottle of DeFiore white wine she'd picked out to complement the meal.

She carried the tray into the dining room and

came to a stop when she noticed the lights had been dimmed and candles had been added to the table as well as some fresh greens and dahlias with hearty yellow centers and deep pink tips. The breath caught in her throat.

The table was perfect. It looked as though it was ready for a romantic interlude. And then her gaze came to rest on Dante. He'd changed clothes. What? But why?

She glanced down at the same clothes she'd worn all day that were now smudged with flour and sauce. She resisted the urge to race out of the room to grab a shower and to change into something that would make her feel sexy and alluring.

She turned her attention to Dante, taking in his creased black slacks, a matching jacket and a gray button-up shirt. Wow. With his tanned features and his dark hair, he looked like a Hollywood star. She swallowed hard. She wondered if he'd remembered to put on a touch of cologne, too. The thought of moving close enough to check was oh, so tempting.

She gave herself a mental jerk. She wasn't here for a date. This was business. She couldn't blow her chance to show him that she was quite competent in the kitchen. She would impress him this evening, but it would be through her culinary prowess and not through flirting or any of the other tempting thoughts that came readily to mind.

"If you'll have a seat, I'll serve you." She tried to act as though her heart wasn't thumping against her ribs.

He frowned. "But I want to get your chair for you."

"You don't need to do that."

"Aren't you joining me?"

She shook her head.

"But you've got to be hungry, too."

She was but it wasn't the food she'd slaved over for the past couple of hours that had her salivating. "I'm fine."

"Oh, come on. You surely don't think that I'll enjoy this meal with you rushing around waiting on me. Now sit."

What was up with him? She eyed him up as she sat in the chair he'd pulled out for her. Was he having a change of heart about teaching her what he knew—in the kitchen, that was?

"I only brought out enough food for one."

"Not a problem." Before she could utter a word, he moved to the kitchen.

This wasn't right. This was not how she'd planned to prove to Dante that she was up to the task of working in Ristorante Massimo. Frustration collided with the girlie part of her that was thrilled to be pampered. It was a totally new experience for her. But it also left her feeling off-kilter. Was she supposed to read something into his actions? The clothes? The flowers and candles? Did any of it have anything to do with their kiss?

When he returned, she gazed at him in the glow of the candle. The words caught in her throat as she realized this was her first candlelit dinner. Romance had never been part of her other relationships. She could definitely get used to this and to Dante—

No. No. She couldn't get distracted again. This was not a date. It was business. So why was Dante acting so strange? So kind and thoughtful?

"Is there something I should know?" she asked, bracing herself for bad news.

A dark brow arched. "Know about what?"

She didn't want to put words in his mouth, especially if they were not what she wanted to hear.

"I don't know. I just wondered about your effort to be so nice."

He frowned. "So now you think that I'm not nice."

She groaned. "That isn't what I meant. You're taking my words out of context."

"I am?" He placed a plate and glass in front of her. "Perhaps we should talk about something else, then."

"No. I want to know why you're in such a good mood. Have you made up your mind about the television show?"

Please let him say that he had a change of heart.

His gaze lowered to the table as he took his seat. "Are you sure you know what you're asking?"

"Of course I do. All you have to do is fill in for your grandfather. And teach me everything you know." Did this mean he was truly considering the idea? Were her dreams about to come true?

"You really want to learn from me?"

She nodded.

The silence dragged on. Her stomach knotted and her palms grew damp. Why wasn't he saying anything?

"Well?" She couldn't bear the unknown any longer. "Where does that leave us?"

"It leaves us with a meal that's going to get cold if we don't get through this first course soon."

"But I need to know."

"And you will. Soon."

Was that a promise? It sounded like one. But what was soon in his book? She glanced down at her salad. How in the world was she supposed to eat now?

CHAPTER ELEVEN

HE MUST HAVE lost his mind.

That had to be it. Otherwise why would he even consider going along with this arrangement?

Dante stared across the candlelit table at Lizzie. He noticed how she'd moved the food around on her plate, but she'd barely eaten a bite. She had to be hungry because it'd been hours since they'd stopped at the trattoria on their way back to Rome.

And this food was really good. In fact, he had to admit that he was impressed. Maybe taking her under his wing wouldn't be such a hardship after all. His solicitor definitely thought it was the least painless course of action. Easy for him to say.

But the deciding factor was when the potential buyer of the *ristorante* had been willing to wait the two months. His solicitor said that they'd actually been quite enthusiastic about the *ristorante* getting international coverage.

But what no one took into consideration was

the fact that Dante was totally drawn to Lizzie. And that was a serious complication. How in the world were they to work together when all he could think about was kissing her again? He longed to wrap his arms around her and pull her close. He remembered vividly how the morning sun had glowed behind her, giving her whole appearance a golden glow. It had been an experience unlike any other. And when their lips had met—

"Is something wrong with the food?"

Dante blinked before meeting Lizzie's worried gaze. He had to start thinking of her in professional terms. He supposed that if he were going to take her on as his protégée, he might as well get started. He'd teach her as much as possible within their time limit.

"Now that you'll be working here, there'll be no special treatment. You'll be expected to work just like everyone else."

"Understood."

"As for the food, the chicken is a little overcooked. You'll need to be careful of that going forward."

A whole host of expressions flitted across her face. "Is there anything else?"

It wasn't the reaction he'd been expecting. He thought she'd be ecstatic to learn that she'd be working there. And that she'd get her television spot. Women. He'd never figure them out. In his experience, they never reacted predictably.

"And use less salt. The guest can always add more according to their taste and diet."

Her face filled with color. Without a word, she threw her linen napkin on the table and rushed to the kitchen.

He groaned. He hadn't meant to upset her. Still, how was he supposed to teach her anything if he couldn't provide constructive criticism? His grandfather should be here. He would know what to say and how to say it.

Dante raked his fingers through his hair. He'd agreed to this arrangement far too quickly. He should have gone with his gut that said this was going to be a monumental mistake. Now he had to fix things before the camera crew showed up. The last thing either of them needed was to start their television appearances on a bad note—with all of the world watching.

He strode toward the kitchen and paused by the door. What did he say to her? Did he apologize even though he hadn't said anything derogatory?

Did he set a precedent that she would expect him to apologize every time she got upset when he pointed out something that she could improve on? An exasperated sigh passed his lips. He obviously wasn't meant to be a teacher.

He pushed the door open, prepared to find Lizzie in tears. Instead he found her scraping leftovers into the garbage and piling the dishes in the sink.

"What are you doing?"

She didn't face him. "I'm cleaning up. What does it look like?"

"But we weren't done eating. Why don't you come back to the table?"

She grabbed the main dish and dumped it in the garbage. "I don't want anything else."

"Would you stop?"

"There's no point in keeping leftovers." With that, she grabbed the dessert.

He knew where she was headed and stepped in her way. What in the world had gotten into her? Why was she acting this way?

"Lizzie, put down the dessert and tell me what's bothering you."

She tilted her chin to gaze up at him. "Why

should something be bothering me? You tore to shreds the dinner I painstakingly prepared for you."

"But isn't that what you want me to do? Teach you?"

Her icy gaze bored into him. The temperature took an immediate dive. "Move."

"No. We need to finish talking."

"So you can continue to insult me. No, thank you." She moved to go around him but he moved to block her.

"Lizzie, I don't know what it is you want from me. I thought you wanted me to teach you, but obviously that isn't the case. So what is it you want? Or do you just want to call this whole thing off?"

"I didn't know we were starting the lessons right away. Or did you just say those things in hopes of me calling off the arrangement?"

"No, that isn't what I had in mind." How the heck had he ended up on the defensive? He'd only meant to be helpful.

"So you truly think I'm terrible in the kitchen?"

He took the tray from her and set it on the counter. Then he stepped up to her, hating the emotional turmoil he saw in her eyes. He found himself longing to soothe her. But he didn't have a clue how to accomplish such a thing. He seemed to keep making one mistake after the other where she was concerned.

"I think that you're very talented." It was the truth. And he'd have said it even if he didn't find her amazingly attractive.

Her bewildered gaze met his. "But you said—"

"That there were things for you to take into consideration while working here. I didn't mean to hurt your feelings."

Disbelief shimmered in her eyes.

He didn't think. He just acted, reaching out to her. His thumb stroked her cheek, enjoying its velvety softness. She stepped away from his touch and his hand lowered to his side.

"Lizzie, you have to believe me. If you're going to be this sensitive, how do you think we'll be able to work together?"

This was all wrong.

Lizzie crossed her arms to keep from reaching out to him. The whole evening had gone off the rails and she had no idea how to fix things. And the worst part was that she'd overreacted. Bigtime.

She'd always prided herself on being able to contain her feelings behind a wall of indifference.

And Dante wasn't the first to criticize her skills. But he was the first whose opinion truly mattered to her on a deeply personal level. He was the first person she wanted to thoroughly impress.

The thought brought her up short. Since when had his thoughts and feelings come to mean so much to her? Was it the kiss? Had it changed everything? Or was it opening up to him in the car? Had their heart-to-heart made her vulnerable to him?

Panic clawed at her. She knew what happened when she let people too close and she opened up about her background. She'd been shunned most of her life. She couldn't let Dante do that to her. She couldn't stand the thought of him looking at her with pity while thinking that she was less than everyone else—after all, if her own parents couldn't love her, how was anyone else supposed to?

Not that she wanted Dante to fall in love with her. Did she? No. That was the craziest idea to cross her mind in a long time—probably her craziest idea ever.

The walls started to close in on her. She needed space. Away from Dante. Away from his curious stare. "I need…need to make a phone call. I…I'll clean this all up later."

And with that, she raced for the door. She didn't have to call Jules, but she did need the excuse to get away from him. It was as if he had some sort of magnetic field around him and it drew out her deepest feelings. She needed to stuff them back in the little box in her heart.

Being alone in a strange city in a country practically halfway around the world from her home made her choices quite limited. She thought of escaping back to the vineyard and visiting some more with Massimo. He was so easy to talk to. He was her friend. But he was also Dante's grandfather. And the vineyard was Dante's home.

Her shoulders slumped as she headed for the apartment. What she needed now was to talk to Jules. It would be good to hear a familiar voice. She made a beeline for her room and pulled out her phone. She knew the call would cost her a small fortune but this was an emergency.

She dialed the familiar number. The phone rang and rang. Just when she thought that it was going to switch to voice mail, she heard a familiar voice.

"Lizzie, is that you? What's wrong?"

The concern in Jules's voice had her rushing to reassure her. "I just wanted to check in."

"But you said that we needed to watch how much we spend on the phone. You said we should only call when something was wrong. So what happened?"

"Nothing. I just wanted to hear your voice and make sure you are doing okay."

There was a slight pause. "Lizzie, this is me. You can't lie to me. Something is bothering you. So spill it."

Calling Jules had been a mistake. She knew her far too well. And now Jules wasn't going to let her off the hook. "It's Dante. I think I just blew my chance to work with him."

"Why? What did you do?"

"I…I overreacted. Instead of taking his feedback on my cooking like a professional, I acted like an oversensitive female." Her thoughts drifted over the evening. "All I wanted to do was impress him and…and I failed."

"Don't worry about him. Just come home."

"I can't do that. Remember, I quit my job. And your tuition is due soon."

"You don't have to worry about that. I don't have to go to grad school."

"You do if you want to be a social worker and help other kids like us." The remembrance of her promise to her foster sister put things in perspective. She couldn't let her bruised ego get the best of her. She couldn't walk away. "Just ignore what I said. I'm tired. Everything will work out."

"But, Lizzie, if he's making things impossible for you, what are you going to do?"

There was a knock at her bedroom door.

"Jules, I have to go. I'll call you later."

With a quick goodbye, she disconnected the call. She worried her bottom lip and waited. Maybe Dante would go away. She wasn't ready to talk to him. Not yet.

Again the tap at the door. "I'm not going away until we talk."

"I don't have anything to say to you."

"But I have plenty to say to you."

That sparked her curiosity, but her bruised ego wasn't ready to give in. She wanted to tell herself that his words and his opinions meant nothing. But that trip to the vineyard and that kiss in the morning sunshine had cast some sort of spell over her—over her heart.

"Lizzie, open the door."

She ran a hand over her hair, finding it to be a

flyaway mess. What was she doing hiding away? She was a foster kid. She knew how to take care of herself. Running and hiding wasn't her style. She straightened her shoulders. And with a resigned sigh, she moved to the door and opened it.

Dante stood there, slouched against the doorjamb. Much too close. Her heart thumped. Her gaze dipped to his lips. She recalled how his mouth did the most exquisite things to her and made her insides melt into a puddle. If she were to lean a little forward, they'd be nose to nose, lip to lip, breath to breath. But that couldn't happen again. It played with her mind and her heart too much.

With effort she drew her gaze to his eyes, which seemed to be filled with amusement.

"See something you like?" A smile pulled at his lips and made him even sexier than the serious expression he normally wore like armor.

"I see a man who insists he has to talk to me. What do you want?"

He shook his head. "Not like this. Join me in the living room."

"I have things to do."

"I think this is more important. Trust me." With that, he walked away.

She stood there fighting off the urge to rush to catch up with him. After all, he was the one who'd ruined a perfectly amazing dinner, nitpicking over her cooking. The reminder had her straightening her spine.

Refusing to continue to let him have the upper hand, she closed the door and rushed over to the walk-in closet to retrieve some fresh clothes that didn't smell as if she'd been working in the kitchen for hours. She wished she had time for a shower, but she didn't want to press her luck.

With a fresh pair of snug black jean capris and a black sheer blouse that she knotted at her belly button, she entered the en suite bathroom that was almost as big as her bedroom. She splashed some water on her heated face. Then she took a moment to run a brush through her hair. Not satisfied with it, she grabbed a ponytail holder and pulled her hair back out of her face. With a touch of powder and a little lip gloss to add a touch of color to her face, she decided that she wasn't going to go out of her way for him.

Satisfied that she'd taken enough time that it didn't seem as though she was rushing after him, she exited her room. She didn't hear anything. Had he given up and disappeared to his office?

Disappointment coursed through her. The fact that she was so eager to hear what he had to say should have been warning enough, but curiosity kept her moving forward. When she entered the wide open living area, she was surprised to find Dante kicked back on the couch with his smartphone in his hand. He glanced up at her with an unidentifiable expression.

"What?" she asked, feeling self-conscious about her appearance.

He shook his head, dismissing her worry. "Nothing. It's just that when I think I've figured you out, you go and surprise me."

"And how did I do that?"

He shook his head. "It doesn't matter."

"Yes, it does. Otherwise you wouldn't have mentioned it."

"It's just that as tough as you act, on the inside you're such a girl." His gaze drifted over her change of clothes down to her strappy black sandals. "And a beautiful one at that."

She crossed her arms and shrugged. "I...I'm sorry for being sensitive. I'm not normally like that. I swear. It won't happen again."

But the one subject she didn't dare delve into was that her appearance was an illusion. Unlike his other women friends, her clothes didn't come from some Rome boutique. Her clothes were hand-me-downs. For a moment, she wondered what he'd say if he knew she was a fraud. Her insides tightened as she thought of him rejecting her.

"Apology accepted." He patted a spot on the black leather couch next to him. "Now come sit down."

It was then that she noticed the candles on the glass coffee table. And there were the dishes of berries and fresh whipped cream and a sprig of mint. Why in the world had he brought it up here?

When she sat down, it was in the overstuffed chair. "I don't understand."

He leaned forward. His elbows rested on his knees. Her instinct was to sit back out of his reach, but steely resistance kept her from moving. She wasn't going to let him think that he had any power over her.

"Dante, what's this all about? Are you trying to soften the blow? Are you calling off the television spot?"

CHAPTER TWELVE

LIZZIE'S HARD GAZE challenged him.

Dante wondered if she truly wanted him to step away from this project. Had she gotten a taste of his mentoring skills and changed her mind? Not that it mattered. It was too late for either of them to back out.

Somehow he had to smooth things out with her. And he wasn't well versed with apologies. This was going to be harder than he'd imagined.

"It's my turn to apologize." There. He'd said it. Now he just hoped that she'd believe him.

"For what?"

This was where things got sticky. He didn't want to talk about feelings and emotions. He swallowed hard as he sorted his thoughts.

"I didn't mean to make you feel bad about dinner." Her gaze narrowed in on him, letting him know that he now had her full attention. "See, that's the thing. I'm not a teacher. I have no experience. My grandfather always prided himself on being the one to show people how to do things. He has a way about him that makes people want to learn. If he hadn't been a chef, he should have been a teacher."

The stiffness in her shoulders eased. "But I didn't make you dinner so that you could teach me. I...I wanted... Oh, never mind."

She clammed up quickly. What had she been about to say? He really wanted to know. Was she going to say that she'd made him dinner because she liked him? Did she want to continue what they'd started earlier that day?

No. She wouldn't want that...would she? He had to resolve the uncertainty. The not knowing would taunt him to utter distraction. And if they were going to work together, he had to know where they stood.

He cleared his throat. "What is it you wanted?"

"I just wanted to prepare you a nice dinner as a thank-you for what you did by introducing me to your family. And...and I wanted to show you that you wouldn't be making a mistake by taking me on to work here. But obviously I was wrong."

"No, you weren't."

"Yes, I was. You made it clear you don't care for my cooking."

He shook his head. "That's not it. I think you're a good cook."

"So then why did you say those things?"

"Because good is fine for most people, but you aren't most people."

Her fine brows drew together. "What does that mean? Do you know about my past? Did your grandfather tell you?"

Whoa! That had him sitting up straight. "Nonno didn't tell me anything." But Dante couldn't let it end there. He wanted to believe that he was being cautious because of the business but it was more than that. He wanted to know everything there was about her. "I'm willing to listen, if you're willing to tell me."

Her blue eyes were a turbulent sea of emotions. "You don't want to hear about me."

"Yes, I do." The conviction in his voice took him by surprise.

She worried her lip as though considering what to tell him. "I don't know. I've already told you enough. I don't need to give you more reason to look at me differently."

Now he had to know. "I promise I won't do that."

"You might try, but it'll definitely color the way

you see me." She leaned back in the chair and crossed her arms.

He wanted her to trust him although he knew that he hadn't given her any reason to do so. But this was important. On top of it all, if he understood her better, maybe he'd have an easier time communicating with her when they were working together. He knew he was kidding himself. His interest in her went much deeper than employer and employee.

"Trust me, Lizzie."

He could see the conflicted look in her eyes. She obviously wasn't used to opening up to people—except his grandfather. Nonno had a way with people that put them at ease. Dante was more like his father when it came to personal relationships—he had to work to find the right words. Sure, he could flirt with the women, but when it came down to meaningful talks, the DeFiore men failed.

But this was about Lizzie, not himself. And he didn't want to fail her. More than anything, he wanted her to let him in.

Should she trust him?

Lizzie studied Dante's handsome face. Her brain

said that she'd already told him more than enough, but her heart pleaded with her to trust him. But to what end? It wasn't as if she was going to build a life here in Rome. Her life—her home—was thousands of miles away in New York.

But maybe she'd stumbled across something.

Whatever she told him would stay here in Rome. So what did it matter if she told him more about her past? It wasn't as if it was a secret anyway. Plenty of people knew her story—and plenty of those people had used it as a yardstick to judge her. Would Dante be different?

With every fiber of her being she wanted to believe that he would be. But she'd never know unless she said the words—words that made her feel as though she was less than everyone else. Admitting to her past made her feel as though she wasn't worthy of love.

She took a deep breath. "Before my mother died, I was placed in foster care."

Dante sat there looking at her as though he were still waiting for her big revelation.

"Did you hear me?"

"I heard that you grew up in a foster home, but I don't know why you would think that would make me look at you differently."

Seriously? This was so not the reaction she was expecting. Growing up, she'd learned to keep this information to herself. When the parents of her school friends had learned that she came from a foster home, they'd clucked their tongues and shaken their heads. Then suddenly her friends had no time for her. And once she'd overheard a parent say to another, *"You can never be too careful. Who knows about those foster kids. I don't want her having a bad influence on my kid."*

The memory made the backs of Lizzie's eyes sting. She'd already felt unwanted by her mother, who'd tossed her away as though she hadn't mattered. And then to know that people looked down on her, it hurt—a lot. But Lizzie refused to let it destroy her. Instead, she insisted on showing them that they were wrong—that she would make something of herself.

"You don't understand what it's like to grow up as a foster kid. Trust me. You had it so good."

Dante glanced away. "You don't know that."

"Are you serious? You have an amazing family. You know where you come from and who your parents are."

"It may look good from the outside, but you have no idea what it's like to live in that house and never be able to measure up." He got to his feet and strode over to the window.

"Maybe your family expected things from you because they knew you were capable of great things. In my case, no one expected anything from me but trouble."

"Why would they think that?"

"Don't you get it? My parents tossed me away like yesterday's news. If the two people in the world who were supposed to love me the most didn't want me, it could only mean there's something wrong with me—something unworthy." Her voice cracked with emotion. "You don't know what it was like to be looked at like you are less than a person."

In three long, quick strides Dante was beside her. He sat down next to her and draped his arm around her. Needing to feel his strength and comfort, she lowered her head to his broad shoulder. The lid creaked open on the box of memories that she'd kept locked away for so many years.

Once again she was that little girl with the hand-me-down jeans with patches on the knees and the pant legs that were two inches too short. And the socks that rarely matched—she'd never forget those. She'd been incessantly taunted and teased about them.

But no longer.

Her clothes may not come from high-class shops, but they were of designer quality and gently worn so that no one knew that they were used—no one but Jules. But her foster sister was never one to judge. Probably because Jules never went for the sophisticated styles—Jules marched to a different drummer in fashion and makeup.

"I…I never had any friendships that lasted, except Jules. We had similar backgrounds and we leaned on each other through thick and thin."

"I'm so glad she was there for you. If I had been there I'd have told those people what was up."

Lizzie gave a little smile. "I can imagine you doing that, too."

"I don't understand why people have to be so mean."

She swallowed down the lump in her throat. "You can't imagine how awful it was. At least when I was little, I didn't know what the looks and snide little comments by the mothers were about, but as I got older, I learned."

Dante's jaw tightened and a muscle in his cheek twitched. "Unbelievable."

"The kids were even meaner. If you didn't have the right clothes, and I never did, you'd be picked on and called names. And the right hairstyle, you had to have the latest trend. And my poker-straight hair would never cooperate. It seemed one way or another I constantly failed to fit in."

"I think they were all just jealous. How could they not be? You're gorgeous."

His compliment was like a balm on her old wounds. Did he really mean it? She gazed deep into his eyes and saw sincerity, which stole her breath away. Dante thought she was gorgeous. A warmth started in her chest and worked its way up her neck and settled in her cheeks.

"It's a shame they missed getting to know what a great person you are. And how caring you are."

She lifted her head and looked at him squarely in the eyes. "You're just saying that to make me feel better."

"No, I'm not." His breath brushed against her cheek, tickling it. "You're special."

She moved just a little so that she was face-to-face with him. She wanted to look into his eyes once more. She wanted to know without a doubt that he believed what he was saying. But what she found in his dark gaze sent her heart racing. Sincerity and desire reflected in his eyes.

He pulled her closer until her curves were pressed up against his hard planes. She knew this place. Logic said she should pull away. But the pounding of her heart drowned out any common sense. The only recognizable thought in her head was that she wanted him—all of him, and it didn't matter at that moment what happened tomorrow.

His gaze dipped to her lips. The breath caught in his throat. Her eyelids fluttered closed and then he was there pressing his mouth to hers. Her hands crept over his sturdy shoulders. Her fingertips raked through his short strands.

She followed his gently probing kisses until her mounting desire drove her to become more assertive. As she deepened their kiss, a moan sounded from him. She reveled in the ability to rouse his interest. Sure, she'd attracted a few men in the past, but none had gotten her heart to pound like it was doing now. She wondered if Dante could hear it. Did he know what amazing things he was doing to her body?

Did he know how much she wanted him?

The knowledge that she was willing to give herself to him just for the asking startled her back to reality. She pulled back. She wanted Dante too much. It was too dangerous. And after being a foster kid, she liked to play things safe—at least where her heart was concerned. She'd been burned far too many times.

"What's wrong?" Dante tried to pull her back to him.

She'd been here before, putting her heart on the line. Only then, she'd been a kid wanting to have a best friend and thinking that all would be fine. Then the parents had stepped in and she was rejected.

She remembered the agonizing pain of losing friend after friend. She'd promised herself that she'd never let herself be that vulnerable again. Not for anyone. Not even for this most remarkable man.

She struggled to slow her breathing and then uttered, "We can't do this. It isn't right."

"It sure felt right to me." He sent her a dreamy smile that made her heart flip-flop.

"Dante, don't. I'm being serious."

"And so am I. What's wrong with having a little fun?"

"It's more than that. It's… Oh, I don't know." Her insides were a ball of conflicting emotions.

"Relax. I won't push you for something you don't want to do."

The problem was that she did want him. She wanted him more than she'd wanted anyone in her life. But it couldn't happen. She wouldn't let it. It would end in heartbreak—her heartbreak.

Dante placed a thumb beneath her chin and tilted it up until their gazes met. "Don't look so sad."

"I'm not." Then feeling a moment of panic over how easy it'd be to give in to these new feelings, she backed away from him. "You don't even know me. Why are you being so nice?"

"Seriously. Are you really going to play that card?" He smiled and shook his head in disbelief. "You aren't that much of a mystery."

She crossed her arms, not sure how comfortable she was with him thinking that he knew so much about her. "And what do you think you know about me?"

"I know that you like to put on a tough exterior to keep people at arm's length, but deep down you are sweet and thoughtful. I saw you with my family and especially Massimo. You listened to him and you didn't rush him when he had problems pronouncing some words. You made him feel like he had something important to say—like he was still a contributing member of the family."

"I'm glad to hear that my visit helped. I wish I could go back."

"You can…if you stay here."

What? Had she heard him correctly? He wanted her to stay? She didn't understand what was happening here. Not too long ago she'd been the one pushing for this arrangement to work and he was the one resisting the arrangement. Now suddenly he wanted her to stay. What was she missing?

"Why?" She searched his face, trying to gain a glimmer of insight.

"Why not?"

"That's not an answer. Why did you suddenly have this change of heart?"

He shifted his weight from one foot to the other. "I've had a chance to think it over. And I think that we can help each other."

"Are you saying this because I told you about my background? Is this some sort of sympathy?"

"No." The response came quickly—too quickly. "Why would you say that?"

She shrugged. "Why not? It's the only reason I can see for you to want this arrangement to work. Or is there something I don't know?"

There was a look in his eyes. Was it surprise? Had she stumbled across something?

"Tell me, Dante. Otherwise, I'm outta here. If you can't be honest with me, we can't work together." And she meant it. Somehow, someway she'd scrape together the money for Jules to go to grad school, to reach her dreams and to be able to help other unfortunate children.

He exhaled a frustrated sigh. "I talked with my solicitor before dinner."

When he paused, she prompted him. "And."

"He said that we could break the contract but it wouldn't be quick or cheap."

Her gut was telling her that there was more to this than he was telling her. "What else?"

Dante rubbed the back of his neck. "Did anyone ever tell you that you're pushy?"

"I am when I have to be—when I can tell that I'm not being given the whole truth."

"Well, that's it. My solicitor advised me that it would be easier to go through with your project. And he mentioned that in the end it would benefit the *ristorante* and bring in more tourist traffic."

So that was it. He was looking at his bottom line. She couldn't fault him for that because technically she was doing the same thing. She was looking forward to the money she earned to help her foster sister. But she just couldn't shake the memories of the past.

"And you're sure this has nothing to do with what I told you about my past."

"I swear. Now will you stay?"

She didn't know what to say. She wasn't sure how this would work now that they'd kissed twice and were sharing an apartment, regardless of its spaciousness. When she glanced into Dante's eyes, the fluttering feeling churned in her stomach. And when her gaze slipped down to his lips, she was tempted to steal another kiss.

"What's the matter?" Dante asked, arching his brow. "Are you worried about us being roommates?"

"How did you know?"

The corner of his tempting mouth lifted in a knowing smile. "Because you aren't the only one wondering about that question. But before you let that chase you off, remember the reason you came here—to learn. To hone your cooking skills."

"But I can't do that if you and I are…you know…"

"How about I make you a promise that I won't kiss you again…until you ask me. I will be the perfect host and teacher— Well, okay, the teaching might be a bit rough at first but I will try my best."

She looked deep into his eyes, finding sincerity. Her gut said to trust him. But it was these new feelings that she didn't trust. Still, this was her only viable option to hold up her promise to Jules, who'd helped her through school and pushed her to reach for her dreams. How could she do any less in return?

With a bit of hesitancy, she stuck out her hand. "You have a deal."

CHAPTER THIRTEEN

WHAT EXACTLY HAD he gotten himself into?

The sun was flirting with the horizon as Dante yawned and entered the kitchen of Ristorante Massimo. The film crew was quite timely. Dante stood off to the side, watching the bustle of activity as a large pot of *caffé* brewed. The large kitchen instantly shrank as the camera crew, makeup artist and director took over the area. In no time, spotless countertops were covered with equipment, cases and papers. The place no longer looked like the kitchen his grandfather had taught him to cook in—the large room that held some of his happiest memories.

Dante inwardly groaned and stepped out of the way of a young assistant wheeling in another camera. So much for the peace and tranquillity that he always enjoyed at this time of the day. He slipped into the office to enjoy his coffee.

"Hey, what are you doing in here?" Lizzie's voice called out from behind him.

He turned to find her lingering in the doorway. The smile on her face lit up her eyes. She practically glowed. Was it the television cameras that brought out this side of her? The thought saddened him. He wished that he could evoke such happiness in her. But it was best that they'd settled things and agreed that from now on she was hands off for him.

"I'm just staying out of the way. Is all of that stuff necessary?"

"There's not much. You should see what they have in the studio."

"I don't remember all of those things when they filmed here before."

She shrugged. "Are you ready for this?"

He wasn't. He really didn't want to be a television star, but he'd given his word and he wouldn't go back on that—he wouldn't disappoint Lizzie. She'd been disappointed too many times in her life.

"Yes, I am. We need to get this done before the employees show up to get everything started for the lunch crowd. What do we need to do first?"

"You need makeup."

"What?" He shook his head and waved off the idea. "I don't think so."

His thoughts filled with images of some lady applying black eyeliner and lipstick to him. His nose turned up at the idea. No way. Wasn't happening. Not in his lifetime.

"Is it really that bad?" Lizzie's sweet laugh grated on his taut nerves.

"I agreed to teach you to cook in front of the cameras, but I never agreed to eyeliner."

Lizzie stepped closer. "What? You don't think you need a little cover stick and maybe a little blush."

His gaze narrowed on her as she stopped right in front of him. The amusement danced in her eyes. He truly believed, next to her visit with his grandfather, this was the happiest he'd seen her. He didn't want it to end, but he had to draw a line when it came to makeup.

"I'm not doing it. And you can keep smiling at me, but it isn't going to change my mind."

Her fingertip stroked along his jaw. "Mmm, nice. Someone just shaved."

Yes, he had. Twice. "That doesn't have anything to do with makeup."

Her light touch did the craziest things to his pulse. And was that the sweet scent of her perfume? Or was it the lingering trace of her shampoo? He inhaled deeper. Whatever it was, he could definitely get used to it.

Her fingertip moved to his bottom lip, which triggered nerve endings that shot straight through to his core. Her every touch was agonizing as he struggled not to pull her close and replace her finger with her lips. But he'd once again given his word to be on his best behavior.

He caught her arm and pulled it away from his mouth. "You might want to stop doing that or I won't be responsible for what happens next."

Her baby blues opened wide and her pink frosty lips formed an O.

She withdrew her arm and stepped back. He regretted putting an end to her fun as she seemed to regress back into her shell. He wished she'd let that side of her personality out more often. But obviously he'd have to get a better grip on himself so that next time he didn't chase her away.

She was so beautiful. So amazing. So very tempting. And he'd been the biggest fool in the world to promise to be a gentleman. But he had no one to blame for this agonizing torture except himself.

"You need to loosen up. Act natural."

Lizzie glanced up at the director, thinking he

was talking to Dante. After all, she'd done this sort of thing before—acting in front of the cameras. But instead of the young guy giving Dante a pointed look, the man was staring directly at her. Her chest tightened.

"I...I am."

The man shook his head and turned to his cameraman to say something.

Dante moved to her side. "What's the matter, Lizzie? Where's the woman who just a little bit ago was teasing me about makeup?"

She refused to let him get the best of her. "Speaking of which, I see that you're wearing some. Looks good. Except you might want a little more eyeliner."

"What?" He grabbed a stainless-steel pot and held it up so he could see his reflection. His dark brows drew together. "I'm not wearing eyeliner."

She smiled.

"That's what I want." The director's voice drew her attention. "I want that spark and easy interaction on the camera."

Lizzie inwardly groaned. The man didn't know what he was asking of her. She chanced a glance at Dante as he returned the pot to a shelf. She wasn't the only one who'd reverted back behind a wall. He had been keeping his distance around her, too. She wondered if he regretted their kissing? Or was it something deeper? Did it have something to do with the reason Dante lived all alone in that spacious apartment that was far too big for just one person?

"Okay, let's try this shot again."

Lizzie took her position at the counter, trying her best to act relaxed and forget about the camera facing her. But as Dante began his lines and moved around her, showing her how to prepare the *pasta alla gricia*, she could smell his spicy aftershave. It'd be so easy to give in to her desires. But where would that leave her? Brokenhearted and alone. Her muscles stiffened.

"Cut." The director walked up to her. "I don't understand. We've worked together before and you did wonderfully. What's the problem now?"

The problem was Dante looked irresistibly sexy in his pressed white jacket. She swallowed hard. As she took a deep calming breath, she recalled his fresh, soapy scent. Mmm…he smelled divine. What was she supposed to do? When he got close enough to assist her with the food prep, she panicked—worried she'd end up caring about him.

That she'd end up falling for him. And that just couldn't happen. She wouldn't let it.

"Nothing is wrong." She hoped her voice sounded more assured than she felt at the moment. "I'll do better."

The director frowned at her. "Maybe you should take a break. We'll shoot the next segment with just Dante."

Lizzie felt like a kid in school that had just gotten a stern warning from the principal before being dismissed to go contemplate her actions. Keeping her gaze straight ahead and well away from Dante, she headed for the coffeepot, where she filled up a cup. After a couple of dashes of sugar and topping it off with cream, she headed for the office. It was her only refuge from prying eyes.

She resisted the urge to close the door. She didn't need them speculating that she'd dissolved into a puddle of tears. It would take a lot more than messing up a shot to start the waterworks.

More than anything, she was frustrated. She grabbed for her cell phone, wanting to hear Jules's voice. Her foster sister always had a way of talking her off ledges. But just as she was about to press the last digit, she realized that with the time difference, Jules would still be sound asleep.

Lizzie slid the phone back in her pocket. What was she going to do now? Dante was totally showing her up in there. The thought did not sit well with her at all.

Since when did she let a man get to her? She could be a professional. She wasn't some teenager with a crush. She was a grown woman with responsibilities. It was time she started acting that way before this whole spotlight series went up in flames.

"Are you all right?" Dante's voice came from behind her.

"I'm fine. Why does everyone keep asking me that?"

"Because you haven't been acting like yourself." Concern reflected in his eyes. "Tell me what's bothering you. I'll help if I can."

"Don't do that."

His forehead wrinkled. "What?"

"Act like we're something we're not." If he continued to treat her this way, her resolve would crack. And she didn't want to rely on him. She knew what would happen then. He'd pull back just like her ex had done. Men were only into women for an uncomplicated good time.

And she was anything but uncomplicated.

"I don't know what you're talking about." Dante's voice took on a deeper tone. "All I wanted to do was help." He held up his hands innocently. "But I can tell when I'm not wanted."

He stormed back out the door.

Good. Not that she was happy that he was upset. But she could deal with his agitation much easier than she could his niceness. Each kind word he spoke to her was one more chip at the wall she'd carefully built over the years to protect herself. And she wasn't ready to take it down for him or anyone.

At last, feeling as though she had her head screwed on straight, she returned to the kitchen. The director looked at her as though studying her. "You ready?"

She nodded. "Yes, I am."

The director had them take their places as Lizzie sensed Dante's agitation and distance. She was sorry that it had to be this way, but she could at last think straight. And when the director called a halt to the filming, it was Dante who fouled up the shot. They redid it a few times until the director was satisfied.

This arrangement may have been her idea, but at the time she hadn't a clue how hard it was going to be to work so closely with Dante. Still, she had to do this. She didn't have a choice. There were bills to meet and grad school to pay.

She just had to pretend that Dante was no one special. But was that possible in the long run? How was she supposed to ignore these growing feelings when she found Dante fascinating in every way?

She was in trouble. Deep trouble.

CHAPTER FOURTEEN

NOT TOO BAD.

Lizzie stifled a yawn as she poured herself a cup of coffee. Thankfully it was late Friday night and the restaurant was at last closed. She was relieved that there was no filming in the morning. Those early wake-up calls were wearing her down. The next morning the crew was off to shoot some footage of Rome to pad their spotlights. And she couldn't be happier.

Lizzie pressed a cup of stale coffee to her lips.

"You might not want to drink that."

She turned at the sound of Dante's voice. "Why not?"

"That stuff is strong enough to strip paint off Red. You'll never get to sleep if you drink it."

She held back a laugh. "Don't worry. I'll be fine."

Dante raised a questioning brow before he turned back to finish cleaning the grill. He really was a hands-on kinda guy. She didn't know why that should surprise her. He'd never once sloughed off his work onto his staff. Everyone had their assigned duties and they all seemed to work in harmony.

Dante had been remarkable when it came to the filming, too. He may grump and growl like an old bear about things like makeup, but when the cameras started to roll, he really came through for her—for them. Maybe he hadn't nailed every scene but he'd been trying and that was what counted. And if she didn't know better, she'd swear he'd been enjoying himself in front of the cameras.

It was amazing how long it took to shoot a short segment to splice into the station's number-one-rated cooking show. But it was so worth it. What a plum spot they'd been given. It'd definitely make her credentials stand out from the competition when she returned to New York and searched for a chef position at one of the upscale restaurants in Manhattan.

She took the cup of coffee to the office and cleared off a spot at the end of the couch. No sooner had she gotten comfortable than Dante sauntered into the room.

"See, you should have taken me up on my offer

to take the afternoon off." He sent her an *I told you so* look.

She shrugged. "I wanted to get a feel for how everything works around here."

"And now you're exhausted."

"Listen to who's talking. You worked just as many hours as I did."

"But I'm used to it."

Now, that did surprise her. What was a young, incredibly sexy man doing spending all of his time at the restaurant? Surely he must have an active social life away from this place. The image of him dressed in a sharp suit filled her mind. And then a beautiful slip of a woman infiltrated her thoughts. The mystery woman sauntered over and draped herself on his arm. Lizzie's body tensed.

"Is something the matter?"

She glanced up at Dante. "What?"

"You were frowning. Is it the *caffè*? I told you not to drink it."

Not about to tell him her true thoughts, she said, "Yes, it's cold. I'll just dump it out and head upstairs. Are you coming?"

He glanced around at the messy office. "I should probably do a little work in here."

She stifled a laugh. This place needed a lot more

than a "little" help. "Have you ever thought of hiring someone to sort through all of these old papers?"

"I don't think there's a person alive that would willingly take on this challenge. My grandfather was not much of a businessman. He did the bare minimum. And I'm afraid that I'm not much better. I'd rather be in the kitchen or talking with the patrons."

She could easily believe that of him and his grandfather. They were both very social people, unlike her. She could hold her own in social scenes but her preference was the anonymity of a kitchen or office.

"Well, don't stay up too late." She headed for the door. "We wouldn't want you having bags under your eyes for the camera."

"Is there an in-between with you?"

She turned. "What do you mean?"

"You are either very serious or joking around. Is there ever a middle ground?"

She'd never really thought that much about it. "Of course. See, I'm not making any jokes now."

"And you're also being serious. You're wondering if I'm right."

Her lips pursed together. Did Dante see something that she'd been missing all along? And was he right?

He stepped closer. "If you control the conversation then nothing slips out—those little pieces of your life that let a person really know you. You can then keep everyone at a safe distance."

Her gaze narrowed in on him. "Since when have you become such an expert on me?"

"I'm good at reading people. And you intrigue me."

Any other time she might have enjoyed the fact that she intrigued a man but not now. Not when he could see aspects of her that made her uncomfortable.

"Are you trying to tell me that you're a mind reader—no, wait, maybe a fortune-teller? I can see you now with a colorful turban, staring into a glass ball." She forced a smile, hoping to lighten the conversation.

"And there you go with the jokes. My point is proven."

He was right. Drat. She'd never thought about how she'd learned to shield herself from other people. When conversations got too close, too personal, she turned them around with a joke. Anything to get the spotlight off herself.

After all this time of putting up defensive postures, she didn't know if she could let down those protective walls and just be—especially around a man who could make her heart race with just a look. But something within her wanted things to be different with Dante. It was lonely always pushing people away.

"I'm just me." She didn't know how to be anyone else. "I'm sorry if that doesn't live up to your idea of the perfect woman."

He stepped closer to her. It'd be so easy to reach out to him—to lean into his arms and forget about the world for just a moment. Every fiber of her body wanted to throw herself into his arms and feel his lips against hers.

"Lizzie, you don't have to be perfect." His voice was soft and comforting. "You just have to be honest with yourself and realize that not everyone is out to hurt you. I won't hurt you."

Hearing those last four words was like having a bucket of ice water dumped over her head. Her ex had said the same thing to her to get her into bed. But when opportunity came knocking on his door, she was relegated to nothing more than an afterthought. He couldn't wait to leave New

York—to leave her. The realization of how little he'd cared for her cut deep.

She wasn't going to fall for those words again.

She stepped back out of Dante's reach.

His dark gaze stared straight at her as though searching for answers to his unspoken questions.

When his gaze dipped to her lips, the breath hitched in her throat. What was he going to do? He'd promised not to kiss her until she asked him to. Would he keep that promise?

Factions warred within her. One wanted to remain safe. The other part wanted to sweep caution aside and lean into his arms. Was it possible that being safe wasn't always the best choice? Was a chance at happiness worth the inherent risks?

Dante cleared his throat. "You better go upstairs now." His voice was deeper than normal and rumbled with emotion. "If you don't, I might end up breaking my word. And a DeFiore never goes back on his word."

She turned on legs that felt like rubber and headed for the door. The warm night air did nothing to soothe her heated emotions. She needed a shower to relax her or she'd never get any sleep tonight. And Dante was worried the coffee would be stimulating. It was nothing compared to his presence.

It was on the elevator ride upstairs that she realized if he had reached out to her, she wouldn't have resisted. She wanted him as much as he wanted her. He didn't have to say the words. It was all there in his eyes. The need. The want. The desire.

Sleep was not something that was going to come easily that night.

What was wrong with him?

Dante got up from the desk in his study and strode to the window. The lights from the city obscured the stars, but he knew they were there, just like he knew there was something growing between him and Lizzie. He couldn't touch it. He couldn't see it. But there was definitely something real growing between them.

She'd appeared in his life out of nowhere. At every turn, she challenged everything he believed he wanted in life. But above and beyond all of that, she brought the "fun factor" back to his life. He enjoyed sharing the kitchen with her. He even went to bed each night anticipating the next morning. What was it about Lizzie that had him feeling things that he'd never experienced before?

Images of her curled up in bed just down the hall from him had him prowling around his study instead of sleeping. The only good news was that there was no filming tomorrow. But it wasn't as if they had the next day off. It was Saturday, the busiest day of the week for the *ristorante*. The responsible side of him told him to go to bed this second or he'd pay for it in the morning. But he didn't relish the idea of lying there in the dark while images of the alluring woman who now shared his apartment teased and danced through his mind.

He clenched his hands as a groan rose in his throat. Pacing around his study was not doing him a bit of good. At least if he went and lay down, his body would get some much-needed rest. If he was lucky, maybe sleep would finally claim him. But first he needed a drink.

In nothing but his boxers, he quietly padded to the darkened kitchen. When he rounded the corner, the door of the fridge swung open and he stopped in his tracks, thoroughly captivated with the sight before him.

Lizzie bent over to rummage through the contents of the fridge. A pair of peach lacy shorts rode up over her shapely thighs and backside. He swallowed hard, unable to pry his eyes away from her.

Then, realizing he was spying on her, he cleared his throat. His mouth suddenly went dry. He hoped when he spoke that his voice would come out clearly. "Something you need?"

Lizzie jumped and turned around. "I didn't mean to wake you."

"You didn't."

She closed the fridge, shrouding them in darkness. Dante moved to switch on the light over the stove. He couldn't get enough of her beauty.

She turned, casting him a questioning stare. "You couldn't sleep either?"

"Too much on my mind." He wasn't about to admit that she was on his mind. Her image had been taunting him. But those images had been nothing compared to the real thing that was standing in front of him.

The spaghetti straps of her top rested on her ivory shoulders as her straight flaxen hair flowed down her back. He didn't know that she could look even more beautiful, but he'd never be able to erase this enchanting image from his mind. He stifled a frustrated sigh and turned to the fridge. He pulled it open but nothing appealed to him. When he turned back around, her intent gaze met his.

Her fingers toyed with the lace edging of her top. "What are you worried about?"

"Nothing in particular." He really didn't want to discuss what was on his mind. "I just came out to get a snack."

He was hungry but it wasn't food he craved. When his gaze returned to her face, he noticed how she crossed her arms over her breasts. It was far too late for modesty.

"You know, you don't have to be so uncomfortable around me." He stepped forward. "I promise I just want to be your friend."

"I think it's more than that." She arched a brow. "More like friends with benefits?"

"Hey, now, that's not fair. I've kept my word. I haven't touched you." His voice grew deep as his imagination kicked into high gear. "I haven't wrapped my arms around you and pulled you close." He took another step toward her. "I haven't run my fingers up your neck and over your cheeks or trailed my thumb over your pouty lips."

Her gaze bored deep into his. The desire flared

in her baby blues. He knew she wanted this moment as much as he did. He also knew that opening this door in their relationship would change things between them dramatically. But that didn't stop him. He'd gotten a glimpse of life with Lizzie in it and he wanted more of her—no matter the cost.

Damn. Why had he given his word to keep his hands to himself? Now all he had to work with were his words. He wasn't a poet, but suddenly he felt inspired.

"I…I thought you said you were going to be a gentleman?" Her gaze never left his.

"I said that I wouldn't touch you—wouldn't kiss you—not until you asked me to. But I never said anything about telling you how I feel."

She took a step toward him until their bodies were almost touching. "And how do you feel?"

His heart slammed into his ribs. He swallowed hard. "I want you so much that it's all I can think about. I can't eat. I can't sleep. All I can think about is you. Do you have any idea how much I want to wrap my arms around you and pull you close? Then I'd press my mouth to yours. I'd leave no doubt in your mind about how good we can be. Together."

She looked deep into his eyes as though she could see clear through to his soul. No one had ever looked at him that way before. The breath caught in his throat as he waited, hoping she'd cave. He wasn't so sure how long his willpower would hold out.

Her head tilted to the left and her hair swished around her shoulder. "Do you really mean it?"

"Yes, I mean it." Second by second he was losing his steadfast control. "You are driving me to distraction. It's a miracle I haven't accidentally burned the *ristorante* down."

Her lips lifted. "You're too much of a professional to do something like that."

"We'll have to wait and see. After tonight, I don't know if I'll ever get the image of you in that barely-there outfit out of my mind." He groaned in frustration. "Talk about a major distraction."

A sexy smile tugged at her lips as desire sparkled in her eyes. Her hands reached out to him, pressing against his bare chest. He sucked in an even breath as her touch sent tremors of excitement throughout his body. Did she have any idea what she was doing to him?

This was the sweetest torture he'd ever endured. It'd take every bit of willpower to walk away from her. But he had to keep his promise to her—he couldn't be like those other people in her life who'd let her down. But he didn't want it to end—not yet.

She tilted her chin and their gazes locked. All he could think about was pressing his mouth to hers. He desperately wanted to show her exactly how she made him feel.

He was in trouble—up to his neck in it. And as much as he savored having Lizzie this close and looking at him as if he was the only man in the world for her, his resolve was rapidly deteriorating. Was this what it was like to fall in love?

Not that he was going there. Was he?

He gazed deep into her eyes, and in that moment, he saw a flash of his future—a future with Lizzie. He wanted her to look at him with that heated desire for the rest of their lives. The revelation shook him, rattling his very foundation and jarring him back to reality.

He shackled his fingers around her wrists and pushed her away from him, hoping he'd be able to think more clearly.

"You're really as good as your word, aren't you?" There was a note of marvel in her voice.

"I'm trying. But if you keep this up, I'm going to lose the battle."

"Maybe I want you to lose."

What? His gaze studied her face. A smile tugged at her lips and delight danced in her eyes. He honestly didn't know if this was another of her tests. Or was it an invitation. With a frustrated groan, he let go of her wrists and backed up until the stove pressed into his backside. He slouched against it. Defeat and frustration weighed heavy on his shoulders.

"Don't look so miserable." She stepped toward him.

When she went to touch him again, he said, "Don't, Lizzie. You've had your fun but now let me be... Please go."

"I don't want to leave you alone. Maybe I want you to pull me into your arms and do those things you mentioned."

His back straightened. "Is that an invitation?"

She nodded. "Dante, I want you just as much—"

That was all he needed to hear. In a heartbeat, he had her in his arms and his mouth claimed hers. She tasted of mint and chocolate like the after-dinner treats they handed out with the checks. He'd never taste another of those little chocolates without thinking of her.

And though the thought of letting her slip through his fingers was agonizing, he had to be absolutely sure that she wanted this, too. With every last bit of willpower, he moved his mouth from hers. "Are you sure about this? About us?"

Her big round eyes shimmered with desire. "Yes, I'm positive."

In the next instant, he swung her up into his arms and carried her back down the hallway to his master bedroom—a room he'd never shared with another woman.

But Lizzie was different. Everything about her felt so right. It was as though he'd been waiting for her to step into his life. Things would never be the same.

But exactly where they went from here, he wasn't quite certain.

He'd think about it later.

Much later.

CHAPTER FIFTEEN

DROP BY DROP…

The icy walls around her heart had melted.

Lizzie felt exposed. Vulnerable. A position she'd promised herself she'd never put herself in again. She rushed downstairs to the restaurant. When she got there she couldn't fathom how she'd found the willpower to leave Dante's side—where she longed to be right now. But she couldn't stay there. She couldn't afford to get in even deeper.

Her time in Italy was limited. In just a few weeks, she'd be preparing to return to the States— back where her responsibilities were awaiting her. And then what? She'd leave her heart in Italy. No, thank you. She had no intention of being some kind of martyr to love.

What she and Dante had was…was a one-night stand. This acknowledgment startled her. She'd never thought of herself as the type to have a fling. And now that the scratch had been itched, they'd be fine. They could go back to being co-workers.

With a fresh pot of coffee, she filled a mug and headed to the office. She had no idea how Dante could stand such a mess. It was the exact opposite of the immaculate study in his apartment, which probably explained why almost everything in here dated back years. And she couldn't find any current invoices or orders. He probably did his work upstairs and left this place as a reminder of his grandfather. Dante must miss him terribly. Her heart went out to both of them.

She knew what it was like to miss someone terribly. Her thoughts strayed to Jules. She wondered if she was still awake. She glanced at the big clock on the wall. It should be close to midnight now. Jules wasn't a partyer, but she was a night owl who had a thing for watching old movies until she fell asleep.

Needing to hear her foster sister's voice to remind her of why she should be down here instead of snug in bed with Dante, she reached for her phone. It rang once, twice, three times—

"Hey, Lizzie, what's going on?" Jules's voice was a bit groggy. "Is what's-his-face still giving you a hard time?"

"I...I just wanted to touch base and make sure things are okay with you." Her voice wobbled. Usually she told Jules everything, but suddenly she felt herself clamming up.

A groan came through the phone, the sound Jules made when she was stretching after waking up. Lizzie smiled. She could just imagine Jules stretched out on the couch. She really did miss her. They were like two peas in a pod. She couldn't imagine they'd ever move far from each other— no matter what happened in life.

"Lizzie, I can hear it in your voice. Talk to me." Her concern rang through the phone, crystal clear and totally undeniable.

This call had been a mistake. How could she tell Jules—that she'd slept with the dreamiest man on earth? She didn't want Jules adding one plus one and ending up with five.

Because there was no way she was in love with Dante. He liked fast cars and beautiful women draped on his arm. She recalled the photos of him with various stunning women hanging in the dining room. The strange thing was she hadn't found any evidence that he was anything more than a caring, compassionate man who appeared to be as commitment-phobic as herself.

"Stop worrying. I'm fine. Dante and I worked things out." Lizzie ran her thumb over the edge of a tall stack of papers. "What's new with you?"

There was a moment of strained silence.

"I had an interview for grad school. Actually, it was an all-day event. They even took the candidates out for a fancy dinner."

"I hope you didn't scare them off with all of your makeup and your black-and-white ensemble," she said in a teasing tone.

Jules sighed. "You ought to give me more credit. Actually, I borrowed some of your clothes. I even received a couple of compliments."

Excitement swirled in Lizzie's chest and had her smiling. "Does that mean you're ready for a wardrobe makeover?"

"Not a chance. I'm good the way I am."

"Yes, you are."

Jules used the makeup and clothes as camouflage—so people couldn't see the real her. But someday she hoped Jules would feel secure enough to move beyond the walls she hid behind. Whereas Lizzie's scars were all on the inside, Jules wasn't so lucky—she had them both inside and out, and she took great care to hide them.

"Anyway, it went really well and I was told unofficially that I got in. But it'll take a bit of paper-work before I get my official notification." There was a distinct lack of excitement in Jules's voice. "Lizzie? Are you still there?"

"Uh, yes. That's great! I knew you could do it. And don't worry about anything but getting through your final exams. I've got everything else under control."

"I can tell you have something on your mind. If you aren't happy there, come home."

"It's not that." And it wasn't even a lie. "I'm just tired. I didn't sleep much. That's all it is."

"Are you sure that Dante guy doesn't have any-thing to do with it?"

"I promise he's been great." Lizzie blinked re-peatedly, keeping her emotions at bay. "If you must know, I'm a bit homesick. I miss my side-kick."

"I miss you, too. But you'll be home soon."

"I know. I'm looking forward to it."

"And here I thought Rome would be your trip of a lifetime. I was worried that you'd fall in love and I'd never see you again."

Jules was so close to the truth. Perhaps she re-ally could use someone else's thoughts. "The truth is, Dante and I...we...umm..."

"You slept together?" The awe in Jules's voice echoed through the phone.

"Yes. But it was a one-time thing. It didn't mean anything." In her heart she knew it was a lie, but it was the reassurance Jules needed to hear to keep her calm before her finals. "Don't worry. I'll be home soon."

And the truth was it wouldn't happen again. They'd gotten away with making love once, but to have a full-blown affair with him would run the real risk of breaking her heart. Already she felt closer to him than any other man she'd ever known.

It didn't mean anything.

Those words smacked Dante across the face.

When he'd woken up, he'd reached out and found a cold, empty spot next to him. He'd begun to wonder if he'd just dreamed the incredible night. If it hadn't been for the impression of Lizzie's head in the pillow next to his and the lingering floral scent, he might have written it off as a very vivid dream. Maybe that would have been best for both of them.

By the time he'd searched the whole apartment, he'd started to panic. Where could she have gone?

Why had she left? Did she regret their moment of lovemaking?

And now as he stood in the doorway with the doorjamb propping him up, his worst fears were confirmed. Lizzie regretted last night. While he was thinking that this could possibly be the start of something, she was thinking that it would never happen again. His gut twisted into a painful knot.

Gone were the illusions that last night meant something special—for both of them. He'd been so wrong about so many things. He knew that Lizzie wouldn't intentionally hurt him. She had a good heart even though she kept it guarded.

Hearing those painful words was his own fault. He shouldn't be eavesdropping. Still, not even Red could drag him away from the spot on the white tiled floor. It was better to hear the truth than to misread things and get lost in some fantasy that wasn't real.

How could he have been such a fool? He couldn't believe he'd given in to his desires. He never lost control like that. But when he'd thought she'd finally let down her guard and let him in, he'd gotten carried away. In the end, it had all been in his imagination.

She had only one goal. To finish her job here

and return to New York. Well, that was fine with him. She didn't have to worry about him clinging to her. That wasn't about to happen. No way.

Finding this out now was for the best. In the end, committed relationships didn't work out for DeFiore men. One way or another, when one of them got too close, they ended up getting burned. Luckily he'd only gotten singed, unlike his father and brother, who'd had their hearts and lives utterly decimated.

Dante stepped into the office. "So this is where you're hiding."

Lizzie jumped and pressed a hand to her chest. "I'm not hiding. And how long have you been standing there?"

"Long enough. A more important question is why did you disappear without a word?" He should leave the subject alone but he couldn't.

His pride had been pricked and it demanded to be soothed. Because his bruised ego had to be what was causing him such discomfort. It couldn't be anything else. He refused to accept that he'd fallen for a woman who had used him for a one-night stand.

Lizzie's gaze moved to the papers on the desk. "I couldn't sleep."

Because she was horrified by what she'd let happen between them. He stifled a groan of frustration. "Something on your mind?"

Her gaze avoided his. "Uhh…no. I…ah, you must have been right. I had too much caffeine last night."

He cleared his throat, refusing to let his voice carry tones of agitation. "And you thought you'd come down here and what? Clean up the office?"

Her slender shoulders, the ones he'd rained kisses down on just hours ago, rose and fell. "I thought maybe I could organize it for you."

"And you were so excited to sort papers that it had you jumping out of bed before sunrise?"

Her gaze didn't meet his. "I like office work."

"You must."

She nodded. "I have a business degree."

He struggled to keep the surprise from showing on his face. Just one more thing to prove how little he knew about her…and yet he couldn't ignore the nagging thought that he still wanted to learn more about the beautiful blonde with the blue eyes that he could lose himself in.

He crossed his arms as his gaze followed her around the office as she moved stacks of papers to the desk. "You know, office work isn't part of the contract."

"I didn't know that we were being formal about things."

"I think it would be for the best. We don't want to forget the reason you're here."

Her forehead crinkled. "If it's about last night—"

"It's not. That was a fun night, but I'm sure neither of us plans to repeat it." *Liar. Liar.*

"So we're okay?" Hope reflected in her eyes.

"Sure." He was as far from "sure" about this as he could get, but he'd tough it out. After all, he'd given his word. A DeFiore wasn't a quitter. "You still want to complete the filming, don't you?"

There was a determined set of her jaw as she nodded. He didn't want to admit it, but he admired the way she stuck by her commitments, even if she didn't want to be around him. But there was something more. He peered closer at her, noticing the shadows beneath her eyes.

"You don't need to waste your time in here." He didn't want her wearing herself out on his behalf. "You should get some sleep since you…you were up most of the night. I don't need you walking around here in a sleep-filled haze."

"I'll be fine. I…I don't sleep much."

He wasn't going to argue with her. If she found some sort of comfort in sorting through this mound of paperwork that stretched back more years than he wanted to know, why should he stop her?

"Fine. Sort through as many papers as you like."

Her brows lifted as her eyes widened. "You mean it?"

"Sure. But I do have one question. How do you plan to sort everything when it's in Italian?"

She shrugged. "I'll muddle through. I took Italian in school."

And yet another surprise. They just kept coming, and without the aid of caffeine, he had problems keeping the surprise from filtering onto his face. He scrubbed his hand over his head, not caring that he was making a mess of his hair.

He noticed the eager look on her face. "Whatever. It has to be done soon anyway if I plan to..."

"Plan to what?"

He couldn't believe that he'd almost blurted out his plans to sell the *ristorante*. He hadn't even discussed it with Nonno. There was just something about Lizzie that put him at ease and had him feeling as though he could discuss anything. But obviously the feeling didn't go both ways.

"Once there's room, I was planning to move the business files I have upstairs in my study down here."

"Understood." She gave him a pointed look. "Before you go, we really should talk about last night—"

"It was late. Neither of us were thinking clearly. It's best if we forget about it. We still have to work together."

Her mouth gaped but no words came out. The look in her eyes said there were plenty of thoughts racing round in her mind, but that wasn't his problem. By admitting it'd been a mistake, he'd beaten her to the punch. That was fine with him.

He refused to think about how she'd discarded him and his lovemaking so readily. Soon she'd be gone. He'd just have to figure out how they could avoid each other as much as possible between now and then.

CHAPTER SIXTEEN

PRETEND IT HADN'T HAPPENED?

Was he kidding? The thought ricocheted through Lizzie's mind for about the thousandth time since Dante had spoken the words. His solution was paramount to pretending there wasn't a thousand-pound pink polka-dot elephant in the room. Impossible.

How could he just forget their lovemaking?

As the days rolled into weeks, he acted as though that earth-moving night had never happened. And he didn't leave her any room to explain or make amends. He only interacted with her on a minimal basis. The easy friendship they'd developed had crashed upon rocky shores. She missed her newfound friend more than she thought possible.

And worse yet, their chilly rapport was now apparent on the filmed segments. The director appeared to be at a loss as to how to regain their easy camaraderie. Their television segment was in jeopardy. And Lizzie couldn't let things end like this—too much was riding on their success.

While spending yet another sleepless night staring into the darkness, she'd stumbled across an idea. A chance to smooth things out with Dante.

Instead of spending another lonely weekend sightseeing while Dante visited the vineyard, she'd invited herself to accompany him to the country. Armed with an old family recipe she'd found while straightening the office and with Massimo by her side, she'd commandeered the kitchen. She would cook the family a feast and in the process hopefully she'd mend a fence with Dante.

"Do you really think they'll like it?" She glanced at Massimo as he sat at the large kitchen table near the picture window.

"Don't you mean will Dante like it?"

The more time she spent with Massimo, the less she noticed his slurred speech and the more he could read her mind. "Yes, I want Dante to like it, too."

A knowing gleam glinted in the older man's eyes. "Something is wrong between you two."

It wasn't a question. It was a statement of fact. She glanced away and gave the sauce a stir. She didn't want Massimo to read too much in her eyes. Some things were meant to stay between her and Dante.

"We'll be fine."

Massimo got to his feet and, with the aid of his walker, moved next to her. "Look at me."

She hesitated before doing as he'd asked. She didn't know what he was going to say, but her gut told her that it would be important.

"My grandson has witnessed a lot of loss in his life. He's also been at the wrong end of his father's grief over losing my daughter. I know all about grief. When I lost my dear, sweet Isabelle, it nearly killed me. It can make a good man say things he shouldn't. It can cause a person to grow a tough skin to keep from getting hurt again."

The impact of his words answered so many questions and affirmed her suspicions. "But why are you telling me all of this? It's none of my business."

"I see how my grandson looks at you. It's the same way I looked at his grandmother. But he's afraid—afraid of being hurt like his father and brother. If you care about my grandson like I think you do, you'll fight for him."

"But I can't. Even if there was something be-tween Dante and me, my life—it's in New York."

"Love will always find a way—"

"Mmm… What smells so good?"

Stefano strode into the kitchen, followed closely by Dante and his father. Their hungry gazes roamed over the counter and stove. She shooed them all away to get washed up while she set the dining room table.

Soon all four men were cleaned up in dress shirts and slacks. Thankfully, she'd had a couple of minutes to run to her room and put on a dress. Still, next to these smartly dressed men, she felt underdressed.

"I hope you all like tonight's dinner. Thanks to Massimo, I was able to cook some old family recipes."

"I'm sure it will be fantastic," Dante's father said as he took a seat at the head of the table.

She wished she was as confident as he sounded. It felt like a swarm of butterflies had now inhab-ited her stomach as she removed the ceramic lids from the serving dishes. This just had to work. She had to impress them—impress Dante.

She sat back, eagerly watching as the men filled their plates. It seemed to take forever. She didn't bother filling hers yet. She already knew what everything tasted like as she'd sampled everything numerous times in the kitchen. In fact, she wasn't even hungry at this point.

But as they started to eat, a silence came over the table. The men started exchanging puzzled looks among themselves. Lizzie's stomach tightened. What was wrong?

She glanced Dante's way but his attention was on the food. She turned to Massimo for some sort of sign that all would be well, but before he could say a word, Dante's father's chair scraped across the tiles. In the silent room, the sound was like a crescendo.

The man threw down his linen napkin and strode out of the room. Lizzie watched in horror. She pressed a hand to her mouth, holding back a horrified gasp.

Dante called out, "Papa."

The man didn't turn back or even acknowledge him.

"Let him go." Stefano sent Dante a pointed look.

As more forks clattered to their plates, the weight of disappointment weighed heavy on Lizzie. Her chest tightened, holding back a sob. This was absolutely horrific. Instead of the dinner bringing everyone together and mending fences, it'd only upset them.

Unable to sit there and keep her emotions under wraps, Lizzie pushed back her chair. She jumped to her feet, and as fast as her feet would carry her, she headed for the kitchen.

Her eyes stung and she blinked repeatedly. She'd done something wrong. How could she have messed up the recipe? She'd double-checked everything. But her Italian was a bit rusty. Was that it? Had she misread something?

Not finding any solace in the room where she'd created the dinner—the disaster—she kept going out the back door. She had no destination in mind. Her feet just kept moving.

The what-ifs and maybes clanged about in her head. But the one thought that rose above the others was how this dinner was supposed to be her peace offering to Dante. This was what she'd hoped would be a chance for them to smooth over their differences. But that obviously wasn't going to happen when no one even wanted to eat her food.

She kept walking. She didn't even know how much time had passed when she stopped and looked around. The setting sun's rays gave the grape leaves a magical glow. Any other time she'd have been caught up in the romantic setting, but right now romance was the last thing on her mind.

She should turn back, but she wasn't ready to face anyone. Oh, who was she kidding—she wasn't willing to look into Dante's eyes and to find that once again in her life, she didn't quite measure up.

When others looked at her as though she were less than everyone else, she could choke it down and keep going. After all, those people hadn't meant anything to her. It'd hurt—it'd hurt deeply, but it hadn't destroyed her. And she'd clung to the belief that whatever didn't destroy you made you stronger.

But Dante was a different story. A sob caught in her throat. She couldn't stand the thought of him thinking that she was inept at cooking—the one ability that she'd always excelled in—her one hope to gain his respect.

And now she'd failed. Miserably.

"Are you serious?"

Dante sent Stefano a hard stare. The main dish Lizzie had prepared was his mother's trademark dish. She only prepared it on the most special occasions.

"Of course I'm serious. Did you see how all of the color drained from Papa's face? It was like he'd seen a ghost or something."

Dante raked his fingers through his hair. "I guess I was too busy watching the horrified look on Lizzie's face. She worked all day on that meal. She wouldn't say it but I know that she was so anxious to please everyone—"

"You mean anxious to please you, little brother."

"Me? Why would she do that?" He wasn't about to let on to his older brother that anything had gone on between him and Lizzie. No way! He'd never hear the end of it. "We're working together. That's all."

Stefano elbowed him. "Whatever you say."

Dante leaned forward on the porch rail and stared off into the distance, but there was no sign of Lizzie.

"I just have one question."

Dante stifled a groan. "You always have a question and most of the time it's none of your business."

"Ah, but see, this does have to do with me. Because while you're standing there insisting that you don't care about Lizzie, she's gotten who knows how far away. So is it going to be me or you that goes after her?"

Dante hated when his brother was right. She had been gone a long time. Soon it'd be dark out. He'd attempted to follow her right after the incident, but Massimo had insisted she needed some time alone. But the thing was she didn't understand what had happened to her special dinner and he needed to explain that it had nothing to do with her. Still, he figured that after her walk she'd be more apt to listen to him.

"Dante, did you hear me?"

He turned and glared at Stefano. "How could I help but hear you when you're talking in my ear?"

"You're ignoring the question. Are you going? Or should I?"

"I'm going."

"You might want to take your car. Hard to tell how far she's gotten by now."

"Thanks so much for your expert advice."

Stefano sent him a knowing smile. "You always did need a little guidance."

They'd probably have ended up in a sparring match like they used to do as kids, but Dante had more important matters than showing his big brother that he was all grown up now. Dante jumped in Red and fired up the engine. He headed down the lane to the main road, not sure he was even headed in the right direction. No one had watched Lizzie leave, but he couldn't imagine that she'd go hiking through the fields in a dress and sandals.

He slowly eased the car along the lane, doing his best to search the fields while trying to keep the car from drifting off the road. Thankfully it was a private lane as he was doing a good deal of weaving back and forth.

Where was she?

As he reached the main road, his worries multiplied. Had he missed her? Had she wandered into the fields and somehow gotten lost? He pulled to a stop at the intersection and pounded his palm against the steering wheel. Why had he listened to his grandfather? He should have gone after her immediately.

A car passed by and his gut churned. Was it possible she was so upset that she hitched a ride from a passing motorist? A stranger?

His whole body stiffened. This was his fault. He'd been so upset by her rejection that he'd built up an impenetrable wall between them. Maybe if he hadn't been so worried about letting her hurt him again, she wouldn't have been trying so hard to impress him and his family—his dysfunctional family. If he couldn't please his father—his own flesh and blood—how was she supposed to succeed?

Dante's gaze took in the right side of the main road, but there was no sign of Lizzie. And then he proceeded to the left, the direction they'd come from the city. That had to be the way she'd gone. He could only hope that she was wise enough to keep to herself and not trust any strangers. If anything happened to her—

He cut off the thought. Nothing would happen to her. She would be fine. She had to be.

And then he spotted the back of her red dress. He let out a breath that had been pent up in his chest. He sent up a silent thank-you to the big man upstairs.

He pulled up next to her and put down the window. "Lizzie, get in the car."

She didn't stop walking. She didn't even look at him. He was in a big mess here. He picked up speed and pulled off the road. He cut the engine and jumped out of the car.

By this point, Lizzie was just passing the car.

She was still walking and he had no choice but to fall in step next to her. It was either that or toss her over his shoulder. He didn't think she'd appreciate the latter option. And he didn't need any passing motorists calling the *polizia*.

"Lizzie, would you stop so we can talk?"

Still nothing. Her strides were long and quick. His car was fading into the background. He should have locked it up, but he never imagined she'd keep walking.

"What are you going to do? Walk the whole way back to Rome?"

She came to an abrupt halt and turned to him with a pained look. "It's better than going back and facing your family."

"Lizzie, they didn't mean to hurt you. It's just… just that your food surprised them."

"I know. I saw the looks on their faces. Your father couldn't get away from the table fast enough. It was as if he was going to be sick." A pained look swept over her face. "Oh, no. He didn't get sick, did he?"

"Not like you're thinking." Dante really didn't want to discuss his family's problems here on the side of the road. "Come back to the car with me. We can talk there."

She crossed her arms. "We can talk here."

"Fine. The truth is your cooking was fantastic."

She rolled her eyes. "Like I'm going to fall for that line."

She turned to start walking again when he reached out, grabbing her arm. "Wait. The least you can do is hear me out."

Her gaze moved to his hand. He released his hold, hoping she wouldn't walk away.

"I'm listening. But don't feed me a bunch of lies."

"It wasn't a lie," he ground out. "The honest-to-goodness truth is your dinner tasted exactly like my mother's cooking. At least that's what I'm told since I never had the opportunity to taste anything she prepared."

Lizzie pressed a hand to her mouth.

"It seems that particular dish was her favorite. She made it for special occasions—most notably my father's birthday. He hasn't had it since she was alive. So you can see how it would unearth a lot of unexpected memories."

She blinked repeatedly. "I'm so sorry. I never thought—"

"And you shouldn't have to know these things. It's just that my family doesn't move on with life very well. They have a tendency to stick with old stories and relish memories. If you hadn't noticed, my mother's memory is quite alive. And Massimo had no clue that the dish was special to my mother and father."

"I feel so awful for upsetting everyone."

"You have nothing to worry about. In fact, you might be the best thing that has happened to my family in a very long time."

Her beautiful blue eyes widened. "How do you get that?"

"My family has been in a rut for many years. And you're like a breath of fresh air. Instead of them going through the same routine day in and day out, now they have something to look forward to."

"Look forward to what?"

"To you."

"Really?" When he nodded, she added, "But the dinner was supposed to be special—for you."

"For me?" He pressed a hand to his chest. "But why?"

"Because ever since that night when we…uhh… you know…"

"Made love." It had been very special for him— for both of them. There was no way he could cheapen it by calling it sex. No matter what happened afterward.

"Uh, yes...well, after that you grew cold and distant. I was hoping that this dinner would change that."

"But isn't that what you wanted? Distance?"

Her fine brows rose. "Why would you think that?"

Now he had to admit what he'd done and he wasn't any too proud of it. "I heard you."

"Heard me say what?"

He kicked at a stone on the side of the desolate road. It skidded into the field. "When I found you gone that morning, I went searching for you. I knew that the night wasn't anything either one of us planned and I was worried that maybe you'd regretted it."

"But I didn't...not like you're thinking."

He pressed a finger to her lips. "Let me finish before I lose my nerve." He took a deep breath. "I'm not proud of what I have to say."

Her eyes implored him to get to the point.

"After I'd searched the whole apartment including your bedroom and found it empty, I panicked. I'd thought you'd left for good. But then I saw your suitcase. So I went down to the *ristorante* and that's when I heard your voice. When I moved toward the office, I heard you on the phone. And when you said that what we had was a one-time thing—that it didn't mean anything—I knew you regretted our lovemaking."

"Oh, Dante. I'm so sorry you overheard that."

Hope swelled in his chest. "Are you saying that all of this time I misunderstood?"

Her gaze dipped. "I wish I could tell you that, but I can't."

Piercing pain arrowed into his chest. His jaw tightened as he took a step back. He was standing here making a fool of himself for a lady who wanted nothing but to put thousands of miles between them.

"We should get back to the house and get your things." He turned for the car feeling lower than he'd ever felt in his life.

"Wait! Please." The pleading tone in her voice caused him to pause. She rushed to his side. "When I said those words, I was in the midst of a panic attack. That night had been so special. It had me reconsidering my future. I didn't know what I was feeling for you. I just knew that I didn't want to get hurt."

"And then I turned around and hurt you by putting so much distance between us."

She bit down on her lower lip and nodded.

Damn. What he knew about dealing with women and relationships couldn't even fill up the thimble his father kept on his dresser as a reminder of his mother. "I'm sorry. I didn't mean to hurt you. That's the last thing in the world I wanted to do."

"I never wanted to hurt you either. Is there any way we can go back to being friends?"

"I think we can do better than that." His head dipped and caught her lips.

Not sure that he'd made the right move and not wanting to scare her off, he restrained himself, making the kiss brief. It was with great regret that he pulled away. But when she looked up at him and smiled, he knew that he'd made the right move. There was still something there. Something very special.

"See. Your dinner was very successful. It brought us back together. Thank you for not giving up on me and for going to all of the trouble to get through my thick skull."

She lifted up on her tiptoes and pressed her lips to his. No way was he letting her get away twice.

His arms quickly wrapped around her waist and pulled her close. It seemed like forever since he'd tasted her and held her. He didn't ever want this moment to end. When she was in his arms, the world felt as if it had righted itself.

The blare of a horn from a passing motorist had Lizzie jumping out of his arms. Color filled her face. "I don't think we should put on a show for everyone."

"Why not?" He didn't feel like being proper at the moment. He had more important things on his mind, like getting her back in his arms. "Who doesn't enjoy a couple—" he'd almost said "in love" but he'd caught himself in time "—a couple enjoying themselves on a summer evening."

"Is that what we were doing?"

Not comfortable exploring the eruption of emotions that plagued him when they'd kissed, he didn't answer her question. Instead he slipped his arm over her shoulders and pulled her close. "How about you and I head back to the villa?"

"I don't know. Couldn't we just go back to the city?"

"But your things are still there."

She didn't move. Then he noticed her gaze

searching out his car that was a ways back the road. In that moment he knew how to get her back to the vineyard.

He jangled the car keys in front of her. "I'll let you drive Red."

Her surprised gaze searched his face. "Are you serious?"

"I'd never joke about driving Red."

She snatched the keys from his hand and started for the car.

"That's it?" He started after her. "You just take the keys and don't say a word. You know I never let anyone drive Red, right?"

"I know. But you owe me."

"And how do you get that?"

"I put up with your moodiness lately." She smiled up at him, letting him know that her sense of humor had returned. "And I didn't complain."

He stopped in his tracks and planted his hands on his sides. "I wasn't moody!"

"Oh, yes, you were," she called over her shoulder. "Worse than an old bear awakened during a snowstorm. You better hurry or you'll miss your ride."

"You wouldn't..."

Then again, she just might, depending on her

mood. He smiled and shook his head. Then, realizing that she hadn't slowed down for him, he
took long, quick strides to catch up with her.

CHAPTER SEVENTEEN

LIZZIE CHECKED HER tattered pride at the door. With her shoulders pulled back, she entered the DeFiore home once again. She didn't know what she expected but it certainly wasn't everyone relaxing. Massimo was reading the newspaper. Stefano was in another room watching a soccer game on a large-screen television. She'd been corrected numerous times that on this side of the pond, it was referred to as football. Not that it mattered one way or the other to her. She'd never been a sports fan.

"See. Nothing to worry about." The whisper of Dante's voice in her ear sent a wave of goose bumps down her arms.

She moved to the kitchen. Everything had been cleaned and put away. "I still haven't seen your father anywhere."

Dante shrugged. "He isn't one for sitting around. He's always complaining that there aren't enough hours in the day."

"I'd really like a chance to talk to him—to apologize."

Dante moved in front of her. "You have nothing to apologize about."

"Yes, I do. I made him unhappy and that's the last thing I meant to do."

"He should be the one apologizing to you. That man always has to have things his way—even if it makes the rest of us miserable."

She studied Dante's furrowed brow and darkened eyes. He wasn't talking about her or the disastrous dinner. There was something else eating at the relationship he had with his father.

Maybe she could do something to help. "Have you tried talking to him? Telling him how you feel?"

"Don't go there." Dante's brusque tone caught her off guard.

She took a second to suck down her emotional response. "Listen, I know there's something wrong between you and your father. When he enters the room, you leave. Your contact is bare minimum."

Dante shrugged. "It's nothing."

"No. It's definitely something. And take it from someone who never knew their father and would have moved heaven and earth to get to know him—you need to fix this thing before it's too late."

"But it's not me. It's him. There's nothing about me that he approves of."

"Aren't you exaggerating just a bit?"

"Not really." Dante raked his fingers through his hair. "But you don't want to hear any of this. Compared to you, I have nothing to complain about."

She worried her bottom lip. In her effort to make him realize how lucky he was to have a family, she'd made him feel worse. "My background has nothing to do with yours. But I would like to hear more about you and your father, if you'll tell me."

Dante stared at her as though trying to decide if she was being on the level or not. The silence grew oppressive. And just when she thought he was going to brush her off, he started to talk.

"We didn't exactly get off to a good start as he got stuck with a newborn baby in exchange for losing his wife. Not exactly a fair trade."

"Still, it's nothing that you can be held responsible for."

"I resemble my mother in more than just my looks. Instead of being drawn into the vineyard like my brother, I got restless. My father didn't understand why I wasn't interested in the family business. We fought about it continually until I moved to Rome."

"And that's where you found your passion for cooking."

He nodded. "I thought I had found my calling until Massimo left. It hasn't been the same since." Dante turned to her and looked her straight in the eyes. "If I tell you something, will you promise it'll go no further?"

She crossed her heart just like she used to do as a kid with Jules. "I promise."

"I'm in negotiations to sell the *ristorante*—"

"What? But why?"

"I figured that it's time I moved home. Make amends. And do my part."

"And you think that'll make you happy?"

He shrugged and looked away from her. "I think it's the best thing I can do for my family. Maybe at last it'll make my father happy."

Lizzie bit back her opinion. She'd have to think long and hard about what to say to him because she didn't have much experience when it came to families. With it just being her and Jules, they'd been able to work things out pretty easily. But this bigger family dynamic had her feeling like a fish out of water.

"Why don't you talk to your father? Tell him your plan."

He shrugged. "Every time I try, we end up arguing. Usually over the choices I've made in my life."

She heard the defeated tone in his voice and it dug at the old scars on her heart. "Don't give up. Promise me. It's too important."

Dante's eyes widened at her plea. "I'll do my best."

That was all she could ask of him. And she believed him. Though she didn't think that selling the restaurant and moving back here was the answer to his problems. But that was for Dante to figure out on his own.

"Now, where did you say I could find your father?"

Was she right?

Dante rolled around everything they'd talked about in his mind as he led Lizzie to the barrel cellar. When his father wasn't out in the fields checking the grapes or the soil, he was in the cellar—avoiding his family. As a young child, Dante resented anything and everything that had to do with the vineyard. He blamed the grapes for his father's notable absence.

But as Dante grew up, he realized it wasn't the vineyard he should blame—it was his father. It was his choice to avoid his children. And though his father wasn't as remote as he used to be, some habits were hard to change.

Dante glanced over at Lizzie. "Are you sure you want to do this?"

She threaded her fingers with his. With a squeeze, she smiled up at him. "I'm positive. Lead the way."

He wanted to lean over and press his mouth to hers—to feel the rightness of holding her in his arms. But with his father close by, Dante would settle for the comfort of her touch. He tightened his grip on her much smaller hand and led her down the steps.

As they walked, Lizzie asked about the wooden barrels containing the vineyard's bounty. The fact that she was truly interested in his family's heritage impressed him. He and his father may not hit it off, but he still had pride in his family's hard work. It was why he showcased DeFiore vino exclusively at the *ristorante*.

"This is so impressive." Lizzie looked all around at the walls of barrels. "And they're all full of wine?"

He nodded. "This place has grown a lot since I was a kid."

"Dante, is that you?"

They both turned to find his father holding a sample of vino. "Hey, Papa. I thought we'd find you down here."

"I was doing some testing." His father glanced at Lizzie. "We do a periodic analysis of the contents and top off the barrels to keep down the exposure to oxygen due to evaporation."

"With all of these barrels, I'd say you have a lot of work to stay on top of things."

"It keeps me busy." His father smiled, something he didn't do often. "Is there something you needed?"

Lizzie glanced at Dante, but if she thought he was going anywhere, she was mistaken. He wasn't budging. He crossed his arms and leaned against a post. His father could be gruff and tactless at times. Dante wasn't about to let him hurt Lizzie's feelings any more than had already been done.

Lizzie turned to his father. "Mr. DeFiore, I owe you an apology for tonight. I'm so sorry I ruined your dinner and…and brought up painful memories. I had absolutely no idea that the recipe held such special meaning for you. If I had, I never would have cooked that meal."

There was an awkward pause. Dante's body tensed. Please don't let his father brush her off as though her apology meant nothing. Lizzie didn't say it, but she wanted his father's approval. And Dante wanted it for her. He didn't want her to feel the pain of once again being rejected.

Dante turned his gaze on his father, planning to send him a warning look, but his father was staring down at the vino in his hand.

The breath caught in Dante's chest as tension filled the room. When his father spoke, his voice was softer than normal and Dante strained to hear every word.

"I am the one who owes you an apology. I reacted badly. And I'm sorry. The meal, it…it caught me off guard. It tasted exactly like my wife's."

The pent-up breath released from Dante's lungs like a punctured balloon. He didn't know what was up with his father, but Dante was thankful he'd paid Lizzie such a high compliment. As far as Dante knew, there was no higher compliment than for his father to compare Lizzie's cooking to that of his mother. Was it possible his father truly was changing for the better?

"I'll try not to cook any of your wife's favorites in the future—"

"No. I mean I'd like you to. I know this meal caught me off guard, but it brought back some of the best memories." His father set aside the vino and reached for Lizzie's hand. "I hope I haven't scared you off. I'd really like you to come back and cook for us. That is, if you'd still like to."

"I would…like to cook for you, that is."

"Maybe next weekend?"

Dante at last found his voice. "Papa, we can't be here next weekend. There's been a change in the filming schedule and they're pushing to wrap up the series, so we'll be working all next weekend."

"Oh, I see." His father turned to Lizzie. "So what do you think of my son? Is he good in the kitchen?"

Lizzie's eyes opened wide. "You don't know?"

His father shook his head. "He never cooks for us. Always says it's too much like work."

Lizzie turned an astonished look to Dante. Guilt consumed him. He shrugged his shoulders innocently.

The truth was that cooking was an area where

he'd excelled and he didn't want his father's ill-timed, stinging comments to rob him of that special feeling. But witnessing this different side of his father had him rethinking his stance.

"We'll have to change that." Lizzie turned back to his father. "Your son is an excellent cook and he's turning out to be an excellent teacher."

"I have an idea." There was a gleam in his father's eyes. "I'm sure Dante has told you that Massimo hasn't had an easy time moving away from the city and leaving the *ristorante* behind."

Lizzie nodded. "He mentioned it. What can I do to help?"

"That's the spirit." Papa smiled. "I was thinking that we should celebrate his birthday."

"You mean like a party."

He nodded. "Something special to show him that…well, you know."

"To let him know that everybody loves him."

Papa nodded. "I'll hire the musicians."

Lizzie's face lit up and she turned to Dante. "What do you think? Would you be willing to bring me back here?"

He couldn't think of anything he'd like more. "I think it can be arranged."

She smiled at him and a spot in his chest

warmed. The warmth spread throughout his body. And he realized that for the first time he was at total ease around his father. Lizzie was a miracle worker.

"Don't worry about a thing." She patted his father's arm. "Dante and I will take care of all the food. Although your son might have to get a bigger vehicle to haul everything."

That was not a problem. Her wish was his command. He had a feeling that this party was going to be a huge deal and not just for his grandfather. He had a feeling his own life would never be the same again.

CHAPTER EIGHTEEN

AND THAT WAS a wrap!

Two weeks ahead of schedule, the filming was over. Lizzie was exhausted. They'd worked every available minute to get enough footage for the studio to splice together for the upcoming season.

And so far Dante hadn't said a word about everything they'd shared at the vineyard. Every time she'd worked up the courage to ask him about it, there was no opportunity for them to talk privately. And it was driving her crazy wondering where they went from here. Technically, she still had another two weeks in Rome to learn as much as she could from him. But her biggest lessons hadn't been taught in the kitchen.

Somewhere along the way, she'd fallen in love with Dante. Oh, she'd been in love with him for longer than she'd been willing to admit. And she accepted that was the reason she'd been so freaked out after they'd made love. She just couldn't bear to have him reject her, so she did the rejecting first. Not her best move.

"Something on your mind?" Dante asked as he strolled into the living room Saturday morning.

"I was thinking about you." She watched as surprise filtered across his handsome features.

"You were?" In a navy suit, white dress shirt and maroon tie, he looked quite dashing. "Only good thoughts, I hope."

"Definitely." Her gaze skimmed down over him again, enjoying the view. "You look a bit overdressed to be heading downstairs to help with the lunch crowd."

"That's because I'm not. I made arrangements so the kitchen is covered today. You, my pretty lady, have the day off." His smile sent her heart tumbling.

To spend with him! She grinned back at him.

She shouldn't have worried. It'd been the rush of the filming and keeping up with the increasing crush of patrons that had kept him from following up on those kisses at the vineyard. She was certain of it now.

"I like the sounds of that. What shall we do with the day?"

"I don't know about you, but I have a meeting."

"A meeting?" The words slipped past her lips.

A questioning brow lifted. "Is that a problem?"

"Umm…no. I just thought we could do something, you know, together." Did she really have to spell it out for him?

The intercom buzzed. Who in the world could that be? From what she'd gathered living here for the past several weeks, Dante didn't entertain much, and when he did, it was down in the restaurant.

"That'll be for me. They sent a car."

"Who did?"

His face creased with stress lines. "The people interested in buying the *ristorante*."

His words knocked her off-kilter. She sat down on the arm of the couch. And here she'd been daydreaming about them one day running the restaurant together. She didn't have a clue how she'd work things out with Jules being so far away, but Massimo's words came back to her: *Love will always find a way.* Now all of her daydreams were about to be dashed.

"You're really going through with it?" Her voice was barely more than a whisper.

"Why do you seem so surprised? I told you I was considering it. And thanks to you, things between me and my father are looking up. It's time I do what's expected of me."

He was trying to be noble and earn his father's respect and love. That she could admire. But at what cost?

"Dante, do you really think that you'll be happy working at the vineyard? After all, you couldn't wait to leave when you were younger. Do you really think it'll have changed?"

His gaze darkened. "Maybe I've changed."

"And you aren't going to miss the restaurant—your grandfather's legacy? Have you even told Massimo?"

Dante's brows gathered. "When I took over the *ristorante*, he gave me his blessing to do what I thought was appropriate with it. And that's what I'm doing."

She knew the decision was ultimately up to him, but if she didn't say something now, she'd regret it—they both might regret it. "Don't do it. Don't sell the restaurant."

Dante grabbed his briefcase and headed for the door. "I've got to go."

"Wait." She rushed over to him. "I'm sorry. I'm butting in where I don't belong, but I don't want you to have any regrets."

"I won't. I know what I want."

And it wasn't working here side by side with her. Her heart sank.

"We'll do something when I get back." The buzzer sounded again. "I really do have to go."

He rushed out the door. She willed him to come back, but he didn't. Deep down she had a bad feeling that Dante was about to make a decision that he would come to regret. But there was nothing else she could do to stop him.

Not quite an hour later, as Lizzie was trying to find a television show to distract her from thinking of Dante, the phone rang. Maybe it was him. Maybe he had come to his senses and couldn't wait to tell her.

"Hello."

"Lizzie, is that you?" Definitely not Dante's voice, but still it was familiar.

"Yes."

"This is Dante's father."

"Oh, hi. Dante isn't here. But I can give him a message."

"Actually, you're the one I wanted to speak to. I wanted to know if you needed any help with the food for the party tomorrow. My sisters have been pestering me to know how they can help."

How in the world had she let Massimo's party slip her mind? Of course, with the crazy filming schedule and the vibes of attraction zinging back and forth between her and Dante, it culminated into a surge, short-circuiting her mind.

"Don't worry about a thing. I have everything under control." No way was she telling him the truth. Not after that disastrous dinner.

"I knew I could count on you." His confidence in her only compounded her guilt. "This party is going to be just what Massimo needs. A houseful of family and friends with great food, music and the best vino."

They talked for a few more minutes before she gave in and said that his sisters could do the appetizers, but the entrées were her and Dante's responsibility.

As she hung up the phone, her mind was racing. That was when she realized they hadn't picked up the collage of photos of the restaurant through the years to hang in Massimo's room at the vineyard. A quick call assured her that the order was complete, but she'd have to get there right away. In twenty minutes, they closed for the weekend. She tried calling Dante's cell phone but it went straight to voice mail.

A glance at the clock told her that she didn't have time to wait. She needed to go right now. She wouldn't let Dante down in front of his family. Not when he was so anxious to fix things with his father. This gift was from the both of them, but it was more Dante's idea than hers.

Spotting the keys to Red on the counter, she wondered if Dante would mind if she borrowed the car. After all, this was an emergency and he had let her drive it when they were in the country. What could it hurt? The shop wasn't too far away.

Before she could change her mind, she grabbed the keys and headed out the door. Her stomach quivered with nerves as she fired up the engine. As she maneuvered Red down the street, heads turned. She could only ever dream of having a luxury sports car for herself. Without even checking, she knew that the price tag on this gem was not even in her realm of possibilities...ever.

In no time, she placed the large framed collage in the passenger seat. Being cautious, she used the seat belt to hold it in place. She didn't want anything to happen to the gift. It was perfect. And she was certain that Massimo would treasure it.

Mentally she was listing everything she needed to start preparing as soon as she got home. The

fact that there would be a hundred-plus people at this "small" gathering totally boggled her
mind. When she and Jules had a birthday party,
it usually ended up being them and a handful of
friends—less than ten people total. The DeFiore
clan was more like a small village.

She would need at least four trays of lasagna
alone. Thankfully the restaurant was kept well
stocked. When they'd talked about the party pre-
viously, Dante had told her to take whatever she
needed and just to leave him a list of what she
used. That was a big relief—

The blur of a speeding car caught her attention. Lizzie slammed on the brakes. Red immediately responded. Her body tensed. The air became
trapped in her lungs.

The blue compact car cut in front of her, nar-
rowly missing her.

Lizzie slowed to a stop. She blew out the pent-
up breath.

Thank goodness nothing had happened to Red.
Dante would have freaked out if she'd damaged
his precious car. The man truly loved this fine
vehicle—

Squeal!

Thunk!

Lizzie's body lurched forward. Her body jerked hard against the seat belt. The air was knocked out of her lungs.

CHAPTER NINETEEN

"THAT'S NOT POSSIBLE. Lizzie wouldn't be out in Red." Dante gripped the phone tighter. "You're sure it was her?" He listened intently as though his very life depended on it. "What do you mean you don't know if she's okay?" His gut twisted into a painful knot. "I'm on my way."

Was it possible his newly hired busboy was mistaken? Lizzie had been in a car accident with Red? The kid didn't know Lizzie very well. He had to have her mixed up with someone else.

Dante strode toward the elevator of the corporate offices after his meeting. He could only hope the hired car would be waiting for him. When the elevator didn't come fast enough, he headed for the stairwell. Lizzie just had to be okay. His feet barely touched the steps as he flew down the two flights of stairs.

After nearly running into a half-dozen people, he made it to the street. The black car was waiting for him. When the driver went to get out to open his door for him, Dante waved him off. There wasn't time for niceties. He had to know if Lizzie was okay.

It seemed to take forever for the car to get across the city. He tried calling her. She didn't answer at the apartment and she didn't pick up her cell phone. Dante's body tensed. Was the kid right? Had she been in an accident? Was she hurt?

Then feeling utterly helpless, Dante did something he hadn't done since he was a kid. He sent a prayer to the big guy upstairs, pleading for Lizzie's safety.

What had she been doing? Where had she gone? And what was she doing with Red? He couldn't come up with any plausible answers. All he could do was stare helplessly out the window as they slowly inched closer to the accident site.

"This is as close as I can get, sir. Looks like they have the road shut down up ahead." The driver sent him an apologetic look in the rearview mirror.

"Thank you."

Dante sprang out of the car and weaved his way through the throng of people on the sidewalk, sidestepping a cyclist and a few strollers. He inwardly groaned. Just his luck. Everyone seemed to be out and about on such a sunny day.

And then he saw the familiar candy-apple-red paint, but his gaze kept moving, searching for Lizzie's blond hair. She wasn't by the car. And she wasn't standing on the sidewalk.

And then he spotted the ambulance. His heart tightened.

Please. Please. Don't let her be hurt.

He ran to the ambulance and moved to the back. Lizzie was sitting there with a stunned look on her face. His gaze scanned her from head to foot. No blood. No bandages.

Thank goodness.

"Lizzie."

It was all he got out before she was rushing into his arms and he nearly dropped to the roadway with relief. As his arms wrapped around her, he realized that he'd never been so scared in his entire life. If he had lost her— No, he couldn't go there. Losing her was unimaginable.

As he held her close and felt her shake, he realized that he loved her. Not just a little. But a whole lot. In that moment, he understood the depth of love his father had felt for his mother. He'd never before been able to comprehend why his father never remarried—why his father kept all of the memories of his mother around the house. Now he understood.

Lizzie pulled back. "Dante, I'm so sorry. I...I—"

"Are you okay?" When she didn't answer right away, his gaze moved to the paramedic. "Is she okay? Does she need to go to the hospital?"

"She refused to go to the hospital."

Dante turned to her. "You've got to go. What if something is wrong?"

"It looks like she's going to be bruised from the seat belt and a bit sore in the morning, but she should be okay."

Lizzie patted Dante's arm to get his attention. "He's right. I'm fine. But..."

"But what?" If she so much as had a pain in her little finger, he was going to carry her into that ambulance himself.

"But Red isn't in such good condition. Oh, Dante, I'm sorry..." She burst out in tears.

What did he do now? He didn't know a thing about women and tears. He let his instincts take over as he pulled her against his chest and gently rubbed her back. "It's okay. I'm just glad you're okay."

He truly meant it.

While she let her emotions flow, he realized how close he'd come to losing her in a car accident. He knew this scene. He'd lived through it with his brother. Stefano's wife had died so tragically—so unexpectedly.

The memory sent a new cold knife of fear into Dante's heart. He'd watched the agony his brother had endured when he'd joined the ranks of the DeFiore widowers' club. Dante had sworn then and there that wouldn't be him. He'd never let someone close enough to make him vulnerable. And that was exactly what was happening with Lizzie. Every moment he was with her. Every time he touched her, she got further under his skin and deeper in his heart.

He had to stop it.

He couldn't go through this again. Because next time they both might not be so lucky.

As though sensing the change in him, Lizzie pulled back and swiped quickly at her cheeks. "Dante, I'm so sorry."

"It's not your fault."

"Of course it is. I didn't ask you…I tried. But your phone was off. And I had to hurry."

"I had my phone switched off for the meeting."

"I'd forgotten. Then your dad called. And there wasn't time to wait. Then this car cut me off—"

"Slow down. Take a breath." In her excitement she wasn't making much sense and he was worried she might hyperventilate.

"The car—Red—it's not drivable. They called for a flatbed."

This was the first time he truly looked at Red. Any other time that would have been his priority. Warning bells went off in his head. He loved Lizzie more than anything in the world. When his gaze landed on the crumpled rear corner panel, he didn't feel anything. Maybe he was numb with shock and worry after seeing Lizzie in the back of the ambulance.

She sniffled. "I can't believe it happened. I was on my way home when this little car cut me off. I braked just in time. Before I could get moving again, I was hit from behind by that delivery truck."

Dante's gaze moved to the nearby white truck. The size of it was much, much larger than he'd been anticipating. The damage could have been so much worse. The thought that Lizzie could have been seriously injured…or worse hit him in the gut with a sharp jab.

"I don't know if they can repair the car but…but I'll pay the bill or replace it. Whatever it takes."

She didn't have that kind of money. Not that he'd accept it even if she did. The only important part was that she was safe. He'd be lost without her. The words teetered on his tongue, but he couldn't vocalize them. Telling her that would just be cruel. He refused to get her hopes up and have her think they were going to have a happily-ever-after ending. That simply couldn't happen.

Stifling his emotions, he said, "I still don't understand why you took the car without asking."

She turned and stared directly at him. "I told you. I tried to call you but it went straight to voice mail. And I couldn't be late. Otherwise they would have closed."

"Who would have closed? What was so damn important that you almost got yourself killed?"

Pain flashed in her eyes. "Listen, I know you're worked up about your car, but I was trying to do you a favor."

"A favor? You call totaling my car and scaring me *doing me a favor*?" He rubbed the back of his neck. His words were coming out all wrong. His gut continued to churn with a ball of conflicting emotions.

Lizzie glared at him. "I told you I'm sorry."

"But that won't fix anything." And it wouldn't ease the scare she'd given him.

The groan of the motor hauling his car up onto the back of the tow drew his attention. The bent, broken and cracked car was slowly rolled onto a flatbed. It was a miracle Lizzie had escaped serious injury.

If this worry and agony was what loving someone was about, he didn't want it. He didn't want to have to care so deeply—to depend on someone. The price of loving and losing was too steep. He didn't care if that made him a wimp or worse. He wasn't going to end up a miserable old man like the rest of his family—with only memories to keep him company on those long lonely nights. No way.

"Stay here." He wanted to keep her in sight just in case she started to feel ill. "I need to speak to the *polizia* and the tow driver."

In truth, he needed some distance. A chance to think clearly. He had to break things off with Lizzie. It was the only logical thing to do. But why did it feel so wrong?

* * *

What was his problem?

Lizzie had never seen Dante in such a black mood. Did he really care about his car that much? She glanced over to see broken bits of the car being cleaned up. Okay. So she had totally messed up today. She knew it was her fault, but did he have to be so gruff? This wasn't the man—dare she say it—the man she loved.

After he spoke with the tow driver and the *polizia*, he returned to Lizzie. His face creased into a frown. "I'll call us a taxi."

There was no way she wanted to spend any more time around him. She already felt bad enough and had offered to pay for the damages. There was nothing else she could do to make things better. "I'd rather walk."

"You aren't up for walking." His gaze wouldn't even meet hers. "You were just in an accident."

His body was rigid. A vein pulsated in his neck. He was doing his best to bottle up his anger but she could feel it. And she couldn't stand it. He hated her for wrecking his car. "Just say it."

"I don't know what you're talking about, but I'm calling a taxi." He placed the call, ignoring her protests. "The taxi will be here shortly."

She wished he'd get it off his chest. If they couldn't even talk to each other, how in the world did she think they were going to have an ongoing relationship? Her mind was racing. She had to calm down. Everything was under control... except Massimo's birthday party.

And that was when she realized that the gift— the whole reason for this illuminating calamity— was about to be hauled away inside Red. Her gaze swung around to the damaged car atop the tow. Anxious to get to the truck before it pulled out, she took off at a brisk pace. Her heeled black boots kept her from moving quicker.

"Lizzie!" Dante called out behind her. "What's wrong? Would you talk to me?"

She kept moving until she was next to the truck. She reached up and knocked on the window. When the driver rolled down his window, she explained that she needed a package out of the vehicle.

"Couldn't this have waited?" Dante sighed.

"No. It couldn't." Lizzie stood there ramrod-straight, staring straight ahead. She refused to let Dante get to her. Instead she watched as the driver climbed up to the car and retrieved the large package.

When the man went to hand it down, Dante intercepted it. "Let me guess. This is the reason you couldn't wait for me."

She nodded. "It's the gift for your grandfather."

The tension on his face eased. It was though at last he realized she'd been trying to do something for him and she hadn't taken his car for a joyride.

When the taxi pulled up and they climbed inside, exhaustion coursed through Lizzie's veins. It was so tempting to lean her head against Dante's shoulder. They'd both been worked up. They'd both said things that they regretted. Everything would be all right when they got back to the apartment.

Satisfied that everything would work itself out, she leaned her head against him. She enjoyed the firmness of his muscles against her cheek and the gentle scent of his fresh cologne. She closed her eyes, noticing the beginning of the predicted aches setting in. But if that was all she ended up with, she'd be grateful. It could have been so much worse.

But she noticed how Dante didn't move. He didn't attempt to put his arm around her and draw her closer. He sat there stiffly and stared out the window. Maybe he was embarrassed about his heated reaction. That was understandable. She was horrified that she'd wrecked his car. Once they were home and alone, they could sort this all out.

CHAPTER TWENTY

IF THERE WAS another way to do this, he didn't know what it was.

Guilt ate at Dante. Though the ride back to the apartment was only a few minutes, it felt more like an eternity. And having Lizzie nestled against him only made him feel worse about his decision to end things. But he just couldn't live like this—always wondering when the good times would come to a crashing halt. And now that he'd had a small sample of what the pain and agony would be like—he just couldn't commit himself to a relationship.

The sooner he did this—laid everything on the table with Lizzie—the less pain they'd both experience. It was what he kept telling himself on the elevator ride to the penthouse. But somehow he was having trouble believing his own words.

It was nerves. That was it. He didn't want to hurt Lizzie any more than he had to. But in the end, this was what was best for both of them. After all, her life was in New York.

Once they stepped inside the apartment, Lizzie moved to the kitchen area. "I'll need to make a list of what we need from downstairs."

"For what?"

"The party. Remember, we're in charge of the food. Your father wants to taste your cooking."

The party where she would be introduced to his extended family—the party where people would start hinting about a wedding. His aunts were notorious for playing the part of matchmakers. That was why he ducked them as much as possible.

Dante sighed. This was all getting so complicated now. "Lizzie, can you come in here so we can talk?"

She rummaged through a drawer, pulling out a pen and paper. "It's already getting late. We really need to get to work on the food prep. You never did say how we're going to get all of this to the vineyard. You know, it might be easier if we'd take the supplies there and prepare it—"

He'd heard her ramble on a few occasions and each time she'd been nervous. "Lizzie, stop!"

She jumped and turned wide eyes in his direction. He felt even worse now that he'd scared her than he did before. He was making a mess of this.

"I'm sorry. I didn't mean to startle you. I just wanted your attention." He walked toward the black leather couch. "Come here. There's something I need to say."

Lizzie placed the pen and paper on the kitchen counter and hesitantly walked toward him. She knew what was coming, didn't she? It was obvious this wasn't going to work. He just wasn't cut out to be anyone's better half. He'd laugh at the thought if he wasn't so miserable.

She perched on the edge of the couch with her spine straight. "Is this about the restaurant? About your meeting today. Did you go through with the sale?"

That was what she thought he wanted to talk about? He scrubbed his hand over his face. "No, this isn't about that."

"Oh. But did you sell it? Not that it's any of my business. But I was just curious because of Massimo—"

"You don't have to remind me. I know that my grandfather put his whole life into that business." And this was just one more reason why he needed to end this relationship. She was already influencing his decisions—decisions that only a couple of months ago he hadn't needed or wanted anyone's input. "No, I didn't sell the place."

"I didn't think you could part with it. It's in your blood. You'd be lost without the restaurant." A hesitant smile pulled at the edges of her lips. "Massimo will be so pleased to know the restaurant is in safe hands. It will make his birthday gift even more special."

The collage. She'd been hurt because of him—because he'd forgotten to pick up the present. Guilt ate at him. An apology teetered on the tip of his tongue, but at the last second he bit it back. Comforting her would only muddy things. He had to end things as cleanly as possible—it would hurt her less that way.

"There's something else we need to talk about." There, he'd gotten the conversation started.

Lizzie sent him a puzzled look. "But we have so much to do for the party—"

"Don't you see, we can't do this? I can't do this." He turned his back to her, unable to bear the weight of seeing the inevitable disillusionment on her face. "We were kidding ourselves to think that we could ever have something real."

"What's going on, Dante? I thought that we were getting closer. I thought—"

"You thought wrong," he ground out. He hated himself for the pain and confusion he was causing her.

"You…you're ending things because I screwed up and wrecked your car?" The horror came across in the rising tones of her voice.

"It's not that."

He turned around then and saw the shimmer of unshed tears in her eyes. It was almost his undoing. But then he recalled the paralyzing fear of thinking that something serious had happened to her. He just couldn't cave in. It would mean risking his heart and waiting for the day that his whole world would come crashing down around him.

"Then it's my past." She looked at him with disbelief reflected in her eyes. "I should have never told you. Now you think that I'm damaged goods."

"I never thought that. Ever." He stepped closer to her. No matter what it cost him, he was unwilling to let her think such a horrible thing. "You're amazing." His fingers caressed her cheek. "Any man who is fortunate to have you in his life will be the luckiest man in the world."

She stepped back out of his reach. "You expect

me to believe that when you're standing there saying you don't want to see me again."

He groaned. "I'm doing this all wrong. I'm sorry. I never wanted you to think this had anything to do with you. You're the most beautiful woman I've ever known." He stepped toward her. "You have your whole future ahead of you."

She moved back. "Save the pep talk. I've heard lines like yours before. I don't need to hear it again. I was so wrong about you."

"What's that supposed to mean?"

"It means I thought you were different from the other guys I've known. I thought that I could trust you, but obviously I was wrong."

Her words were like spears that slammed into his chest. He didn't know it was possible to feel this low. He deserved every painful word she spewed at him. And more...

To keep from reaching out to her, he stuffed his hands in his pockets. "Don't you get it? I don't do well with long-term commitments."

She waved off his words. "Save it. I don't need to hear this. I have packing to do."

There was still the surprise party to deal with and Lizzie was in charge. But after the accident, he couldn't imagine that she'd be up for any part of it. Still, he couldn't just disinvite her. "What about Massimo's party?"

Her gaze lifted to meet his. "Are you serious? You really expect me to go and pretend that everything is okay between you and me?" She shook her head, her long blond hair swishing over her shoulder. "That party is for your family—something I'll never be."

His gaze dropped to the black plush rug with a white swirl pattern. He choked down the lump in his throat. "What should I tell everyone?"

She gave him a hard, cold stare. "This one is all on you. I'm sure you'll figure something out." She strode off down the hallway. Without even bothering to turn around, she called out, "Don't worry. I'll be gone before you return to the city."

Her back was ramrod-stiff and her shoulders were rigid. He tried to console himself with the knowledge that she'd be better off without him. The fate of women who fell in love with a DeFiore was not good. Not good at all.

CHAPTER TWENTY-ONE

HE COULDN'T BRING himself to celebrate.

Dante worked his way to a corner on the patio. There was no quiet place to hide. The musicians his father hired didn't know how to keep the volume down. And the cacophony of voices and laughter grated on Dante's taut nerves.

It didn't matter who he ran into, they asked about Lizzie. It was as though he and Lizzie were expected to head for the nearest altar as soon as possible. When he explained that Lizzie was returning to the States, they all sent him an accusing look.

He should be relieved. He had his utter freedom back. No chance that he could get hurt and grow old, miserable and alone like his grandfather, father and Stefano. No taking part in the DeFiore legacy. So why did he feel so miserable?

Dante could barely hear his own thoughts. There was nothing quiet about the DeFiore family. Everyone spoke over everyone else, hands gestured for emphasis and laughter reigned supreme. Lizzie would have loved being part of such a big gathering. And she'd have fit right in.

"How's the *ristorante*?"

Dante turned to find his father standing behind him, puffing on a cigar. Dante hadn't even heard him approach.

"It's good." Now that the decision had been made, he decided to let his father in on it. "There was an offer to buy the *ristorante*. It was made by some outfit looking to expand their portfolio."

"Are you going to accept?"

It was good to talk with someone about something other than Lizzie and his failed relationship. "I thought about it. I considered selling and moving home to help with the vineyard."

His father's bushy brows rose. "You'd want to come back after you fought so hard to get out of here?"

Dante shrugged. "I thought it'd make things easier for you."

"I don't need you to make things easier for me." His father's tone was resilient. "I take it you came to your senses and turned down the offer."

Dante considered telling him that they wanted the family recipes as part of the deal but that he just couldn't go through with it. No amount of money could compensate for giving away those family secrets. Some things weren't meant to be shared. But that wasn't the real reason he'd ended up turning down the offer.

Dante nodded his head. "I almost went through with it. But in the end, I couldn't do it."

"What changed your mind?"

"Lizzie." Her name slipped quietly over his lips as the pain of loss overwhelmed him.

"You were planning to run the place with her by your side? Like your grandparents had done?"

Dante didn't trust his voice at that moment. He merely nodded.

"Then why are you here alone? Why did you let her get away?"

His father always thought he failed at things. Well, this time his father was wrong. "I didn't let her get away. I pushed her away."

"What? But why would you do that?" His father put out his cigar in a nearby ashtray before approaching Dante. "Let's walk."

Dante really didn't want a lecture from his father, but what did it matter? He couldn't be more miserable. His father led him off toward the vines.

When people wanted to be alone, the vines always offered solace.

"Son, I know you never had a chance to know your mother, but she was an amazing woman. You remind me a lot of her. I know if she were here she'd insist that I give you some advice—"

"Papa, I don't need advice. I know what I'm doing. I won't end up like you." He realized too late that he'd said too much.

"You sent Lizzie away so you wouldn't end up miserable and alone like your old man, is that it?"

Dante couldn't deny it, so he didn't say anything. He kept his head low and concentrated on the path between the vines, which was barely wide enough for them to walk side by side.

"I'll admit it," his father said. "I didn't handle your mother's death well. I never expected to be alone with two young boys to raise. I…I was scared. And…I took my anger and frustration out on you. I'm sorry. You didn't deserve it. Not at all."

What did Dante say to that? *You're right* didn't seem appropriate. *No big deal* wouldn't work either because it was a big deal—a huge deal.

"If you had to do it over again—falling in love with Mama—would you?"

"Even knowing how things would end, I'd still have pursued your mother. She was amazing. When she smiled the whole world glowed. Loving your mother was one of the best parts of my life."

"But you…you always look so sad when anyone mentions her."

"And that's where I messed up. I closed myself off from life. I dwelled so much on my loss—my pain—that I couldn't see clearly. I missed seeing what I was doing to my family."

"Is that why you never married again?"

Papa nodded. "I was too consumed with what I'd lost to see anything in front of me." He ran a hand over his face. "I can't go back and change any of it. My only hope is that you boys don't make the same mistakes. Love is like life—it's a gift not to be squandered."

Dante studied his father's face, trying to decide if his father was being on the level with him. "Are you serious? You'd be willing to give love another try?"

"If the right woman came along. What about you? Do you love Lizzie?"

Dante's heart pounded out the answer before he could find the words. He nodded. "But how do

I live knowing that something might happen to her? That someday I might be alone?"

His father gripped his shoulder. "You don't. You just have to cherish the time you have together. No one knows the future. But by running from love, you're going to end up old and alone anyway."

Dante hadn't thought of it that way. In fact, if it weren't for Lizzie, he wouldn't be having this conversation with his father. Somehow Lizzie had worked her magic and reconnected him with his family.

His father cleared his throat. "Here's something else for you to consider. You've always known you're different from me and your brother. It's your mother's genes coming out in you. I know sometimes that drove a wedge between us. But that doesn't mean that I love you any less. Sometimes being different is a good thing."

Really? And here he'd been punishing himself for being so different from his father and brother. But if he differed from them in his choice of professions, why couldn't he be different when it came to love? Maybe there was a chance his story would end differently than theirs.

"Now, what are you doing standing here talking to me?" His father gave him a pointed stare, like when he was a boy and had forgotten to do his chores. "Go after the woman you love."

Dante turned to the villa when he realized that he didn't have his car. And the next train was hours away. He didn't have time to waste if he was going to catch Lizzie and beg her forgiveness.

"Hey, Papa, can I borrow the truck?"

His father reached into his pants pocket and pulled out a key ring. "You know it's not fancy like that sports car of yours."

"That's okay. I've learned that sort of stuff isn't what makes a person happy."

Lizzie had taught him that lesson.

Now he had to track her down, even if it meant flying to New York. He'd beg her forgiveness. Whatever it took, he'd do it.

Maybe he and his father weren't all that different after all.

CHAPTER TWENTY-TWO

HOW COULD SHE have let herself get caught up in a dream?

That was what this whole trip had been—one amazing dream. And now Lizzie had awakened to the harsh glare of reality. The truth was no matter how much she wanted to believe that Dante was changing, he was never going to be willing to let his guard down enough to let her in—even if she'd foolishly let him into her heart.

After Dante had left, she'd spent the night lying in the dark reliving her memories of Dante—memories that she'd treasure for a lifetime. Because no matter how the fairy tale ended, it'd still been a dream come true—falling in love under the Italian sky and kissing the man of her dreams in a breathtaking vineyard.

Tears streamed down her cheeks as she called the taxi service to take her to the airport. She took one last look around the apartment, but she couldn't bring herself to walk down the hallway to the master suite. Some memories were still too raw for her to delve into.

With the front door secure, she made her way down to the restaurant. With it being Sunday, it was closed. Maybe she had time to slip inside and—what? Remember the time she'd spent there with Dante? No, that wasn't a good idea. There was only so much pain she could take.

Would that taxi ever show up?

At the sound of an approaching vehicle, she turned. She frowned when all she saw was an old truck ambling down the road. Needing something to distract her, she reached into her purse and pulled out her cell phone. She'd been putting off calling Jules for as long as possible. Her foster sister would be full of questions as soon as she learned that Lizzie was catching an earlier flight than was planned.

Her fingers hovered over the keypad. How was she going to explain this?

"Hey, are you here for the hostess position?" came a familiar voice from behind her.

Lizzie spun around to find Dante leaning against an old truck. "What are you doing here? I mean, what are you doing back so soon? Is the party over already? You did have the party, didn't you?"

She was nervously rambling and he was smiling. Smiling? Why was he smiling? The last time she saw him, he'd looked miserable.

"The party is probably still in full swing. Once my family gets started, it goes on and on."

"That's good." She didn't want to think that anything she did would ruin this special day for Massimo. "I...I'll be out of your way in just a minute."

"Don't go."

"What?" Surely she hadn't heard him correctly.

Before Dante could repeat himself, a taxi pulled over to the curb. She should feel relieved, but she didn't. Whatever Dante's reason was for returning early, it was none of her business. He'd made that abundantly clear before he left yesterday.

Lizzie turned and slung her purse over one shoulder and her carry-on over the other shoulder. She grabbed the handle of her suitcase and turned in time to see Dante leaning in the window of the taxi, handing over a wad of cash. What in the world?

As she approached them, Dante straightened and the taxi pulled out.

"Hey! Wait!" She was going to miss her flight. The last one for the day. She turned on Dante. "What did you go and do that for?"

"We need to talk."

She frowned. She wasn't up for another battle of words. She was bruised and wounded from their last go-round. All she wanted was to be alone to lick her wounds. "There's nothing left to say."

"I'm sorry."

His words caused the breath to catch in her throat. This time she was certain about what she heard. But whether he was talking about how he'd dumped her or whether he was referring to dismissing the taxi, she wasn't sure.

"About what?"

"Let's go inside and talk." He moved to the restaurant door and unlocked it. When he held it open for her, she didn't move. "I promise that if you hear me out and you don't like what I have to say that I'll drive you to the airport myself."

She glanced at her wristwatch. "You've got five minutes."

"Fair enough."

She must be losing her grip on reality. What other reason would there be for her to agree to put herself through more heartache and pain?

Her feet felt as though they were weighed down as she walked inside the oh-so-familiar restaurant. She really was going to miss this place and the amazing people that she'd gotten to know here—most of all, she'd miss Dante.

She stopped by the hostess desk and turned to him. "What is it you want?"

"You."

"What?" Her lack of sleep was not helping her make sense of what he was telling her.

"I want you, Lizzie. I love you."

Her heart tripped over itself. She'd been waiting for so long to hear those words, but before she went flying into his arms, she needed to understand. "But what about yesterday?"

"I panicked. When I got a phone call telling me that you'd been in an accident, I overreacted. It seems like the DeFiore men are destined to grow old alone and I thought— Well, it doesn't matter. All I could think about is that if I lost you I'd be devastated and unable to go on."

Really? No one had ever cared about her that much.

"But if you felt that way, how were you able to just dump me?"

"I thought that by protecting myself that I

wouldn't be hurt. But my father pointed out the fallacy of my logic—"

"Your father? You two were discussing me?" She wasn't so sure how she felt about that detail.

"Thanks to you, we had a talk that was long overdue." He looked around at the restaurant and then back at her. "You opened my eyes to a lot of things including how much I love this place...especially with you by my side."

Her heart tap-danced in her chest. "Do you really mean that?"

He peered deep into her eyes. "I love you with all my heart. And I would be honored if you'd consider staying here and running Massimo's with me."

"I couldn't think of anything I'd like more."

He stepped closer and wrapped his arms around her. "I promise no more panic attacks as long as you promise not to take up skydiving."

"Now that's a promise I can readily make." She smiled up at him as she slipped her arms up over his shoulders. "I'm scared of heights."

"So we're partners?"

She nodded. "But I think we should kiss to make it official."

"I think you're right."

His head dipped. Their lips met and the rest of the world slipped away.

At last Lizzie was home.

EPILOGUE

A month later

THE CLINK OF champagne flutes sounded in the empty dining room.

"To the most amazing man." Lizzie stared into the eyes of the only man she'd ever loved. "I love you."

"I love you, too." Dante pressed a kiss to her lips that promised more to follow. And soon.

"Can you believe we were on television? Our grand premiere." Lizzie couldn't keep a silly grin from her face.

"And you were amazing."

She waved off his over-the-top compliment. "I think those bubbles are going to your head."

"Nope. It's just you."

"Can you be serious for just a minute?"

The truth was that she had never been this deliriously happy in her entire life. Even the evenings she'd spent sitting next to Dante on the couch watching soccer…erm, football made her smile. And she never thought she'd ever appreciate sports, but Dante was opening her eyes to football and so much more.

"I can be serious. As long as it doesn't take too long." His gaze dipped to her lips.

When he started to lean forward, Lizzie held out her hands. "Dante, do you think of anything else?"

A lazy smile pulled at his lips. "Not if I can help it."

"Well, try for just a second."

His tempting lips pursed together. "What's on your mind?"

"What do you think about the television studio's offer to give us our own show?" They'd just received the call and Lizzie was too excited to trust her own reactions.

"I can think of something I'd like better."

She searched his face to see if his mind was still in the bedroom, but his expression was totally serious. "What is it?"

"How about you become my partner?"

"Well, of course I'll be your partner. That's what the studio is interested in. You and me working together—"

"No, I don't mean that." He took her hand in his and looked deep into her eyes, making her heart skip a beat. Then he dropped to his knee. "I mean I want you to be my family."

The breath hitched in her throat as tears of joy obscured the view of the man she loved with all of her heart. She blinked and the tears splashed onto her cheeks. With effort she swallowed the lump of giddy emotion in her throat.

"I can't think of anything I'd like better."

He got to his feet and encased her face in his palms. "I'm sorry I'm unprepared but I hadn't been planning to propose tonight. I've been playing it over and over in my mind. And I just couldn't wait any longer."

She stood up on her tiptoes and pressed her lips to his. Her heart thumped with excitement. She didn't know how it was possible but she'd swear with every kiss it just kept getting better and better.

When Dante pulled away, she pouted. He smiled and shook his head. "I take it that was a yes?"

"Most definitely."

"I have one more serious question."

"Well, ask it so we can get back to the good stuff."

He laughed and she grinned.

"I have an idea and I don't know how you'll feel about it, but what about having the wedding at the vineyard?"

She couldn't think of a more romantic spot on the entire earth. "I love it but…"

"But what?"

"What about Jules?" The thought of being permanently separated from her foster sister dimmed her excitement. "She's my only family—"

"Not anymore—I'll be your family, too. And Jules is always welcome here."

"But she has grad school. I won't let her give up. She's worked too hard for this. I want her to reach for her dreams."

"And she will. We'll make sure of it."

"But how?"

Dante pressed a finger to her lips. "Shh… Nonno always says, *Where there's a will, there's a way.*"

Lizzie's mind and heart were racing. The two people she loved most in this world were divided by an ocean. "I don't know."

"Look at me." Dante's gaze caught and held hers. "Do you love me?"

Without any hesitation she uttered, "With all of my heart."

"Then believe in us—in the power of our love. Believe that the future will work out for all of us. Maybe not in the way we'd expect, but sometimes the unexpected is just what people need. There's a way to make this work with Jules and we'll find it. Do you believe me?"

"I do."

He pressed his lips to hers and the worries faded away.

Together, they could do anything.

* * * * *

Don't miss the second in Jennifer Faye's fabulous THE DEFIORE BROTHERS *duet,* BEST MAN FOR THE BRIDESMAID, *coming August 2015.*

MILLS & BOON®
Large Print – July 2015

THE TAMING OF XANDER STERNE
Carole Mortimer

IN THE BRAZILIAN'S DEBT
Susan Stephens

AT THE COUNT'S BIDDING
Caitlin Crews

THE SHEIKH'S SINFUL SEDUCTION
Dani Collins

THE REAL ROMERO
Cathy Williams

HIS DEFIANT DESERT QUEEN
Jane Porter

PRINCE NADIR'S SECRET HEIR
Michelle Conder

THE RENEGADE BILLIONAIRE
Rebecca Winters

THE PLAYBOY OF ROME
Jennifer Faye

REUNITED WITH HER ITALIAN EX
Lucy Gordon

HER KNIGHT IN THE OUTBACK
Nikki Logan